Seeing Beings is Believing

Chronicles

A Dynasty of Cat People Part 1

Book 1

E & K. Kim

Seeing Beings is Believing Chronicles

Book 1
A Dynasty of Cat People Part 1

By E. & K. Kim.
Aka The Sisters Kim
Illustrated by E & K. Kim

E & K. Kim
Seeing Beings is Believing Chronicles - Book 1 - A Dynasty of Cat People Part 1
ISBN: 978-1-7638491-0-5

About the Authors

E & K. Kim were born in Box Hill Victoria, Australia. At a young age, both sisters were interested in fantasy genres. As they got older they became even more captured by different books and movies. They started to write their own stories about beings such as vampires, wolves and creatures that are mentioned very often in popular culture.

E & K. Kim live together on a farm with their animals. They love the rural aspect that comes with living on a large property. Still being young themselves, they wanted to create a book that contained a collection of stories that aren't heard of except inside these stories that intertwine with each other.

Both sisters wish they could have read a book like this when they were younger. However, now that they get the chance to write their own stories, they hope that everyone, especially younger people never lose their creativity or the imagination they had during childhood. They both believe imagination is the key to creativity and without it the world would be a duller place. Belief in yourself and belief in something is what led E & K. Kim to come up with the Seeing Beings is Believing Chronicles.

You see what you wanna see, you do what you wanna do, you think what you wanna think.
Every story has a connection, and that is the link.

Table of Contents:

Magical Beings here and there.
Hidden Creatures everywhere.
Show your true identity.
As you are now real to me.

Map & Mythical Creature Glossary

Banshees - Country of origin: Ireland (E.g. Thomasin Dullahan)

Bunyip People - Country of origin: Australia

Succubus/Incubus - Species of demons known to fool humans. Also able to remove energy from lifeforms and magical objects/items. Country of origin: Middle East (E.g. Aisha Gregory)

Vampires - Country of origin: First Vampires originated from the Middle East (E.g. Isabella Drusillia)

Cat People - Country of origin: Egypt; also migrated to Australia and South America, see brown spots on the map, (E.g. Cleopatra Philopator)

Zomon - Zombie/Demon Hybrid created to serve demons. Place of origin: the Underworld (E.g. Groady)

Pookas - Species of waterhorse. Country of origin: Ireland

Nickurs - Species of waterhorse from Northern countries. Country of origin: All of Scandinavia

Kelpies - Species of waterhorse originally from Scotland. Country of origin: Scotland

The Ancients - Country or place of origin: Unknown

Werewolves - Country of origins: Stories based from many countries indicate that werewolves originate from and/or have no single country from where they are believed to originate. As they are popular in many cultures around the world. (E.g. Siegfried)

Witches - Country of origin: Universal mythical being. Known throughout the world and all witches are governed by the Witches Covenant.

Mute Beings (or aka as mutants. Beings that were born of a human bloodline with some or little mythical being gene. The type of mute beings with genes or which circumstances they were born from vary depending on the types of the mythical being gene they have.) (E.g. FOG and Levi Virazio)

Merwolf - Country of origin: None since they are a hybrid species. (E.g. Arianna Solaris)

7

Will-o-wisps - Country of origin: England (E.g. Lord Gruesome)

Headless Horseman - Creature similar to the Dullahan. Country known to be of origin: North America also known to Ireland

Ghosts - Spirits are well known around the whole world.

Fae species - (Fairies, types vary) Country of origin: No specifics

Demons - Many demons lurk in the Underworld. Origin point of demons: the Underworld (Ruler of the Hidden Empire; located in the Underworld, the Demon King)

Meerpeople - Creatures of the sea. Place believed to be origin: Atlantis/no specifics (Poseidon, King of Atlantis)

Elves - Species of beings similar to the Fae. Country of origin: Specifically based in Europe.

Dullahan - Being that runs amok at night, creating disturbances/destroying anything in its path. Country of origin: Ireland

Kitsunes - Country of origin: Japan

Hu-Hsien - Species similar to the Kitsune. Country of origin: China

Celtic Wolf - Country of origin: Germany (E.g. Fane Halfdan)

Dragons - Ancient beings worshipped around the world especially (All Asian countries, Europe)

Phoenixes - Country of origin: There are many countries that mention Phoenixes in their cultures such as (Europe, Middle East, Asia, India) (E.g. Jamari Acchamba)

Grim Reaper/Reaper associates - Country of origin: England (E.g. Thomas Reap, Lara Kraft)

Gargoyles - Statues that tend to hang around places of worship such as churches. However, they do not serve the church as one thinks. Maybe priests serve the Gargoyles. Country of origin: France (E.g. Laurent the Gargoyle)

A Dynasty of Cat People Part 1

64 BC, Cairo, Egypt:

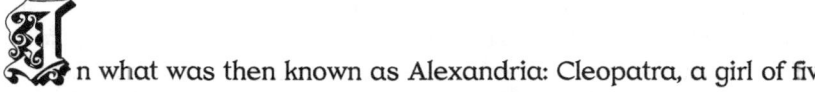

n what was then known as Alexandria: Cleopatra, a girl of five,
was looking out over the horizon; she could see people carrying
goods and flour. They were also trading animals down in what
seemed to be some sort of market. Cleo could hear the chitter-chatter
of the people or smell and almost even taste the spices that the market
people were bartering or selling. The sun was now glistening down on
the pyramids, and soon, the sun would set under the never-ending sand
dunes. As always, it was time for bed, but someone or something was
moving toward Cleopatra. Cleo was still standing in front of the balcony
when her rascal sister Berenice gave her a fright she would never forget.
Berenice threw a snake on Cleo.
'Aaah! How can you do this!' Cleo screamed.

Cleo never had a chance of winning against her mean and overconfident
older sister.
'It's not as if the snake was poisonous! Ha!' Berenice would start
fights over the simplest of things, and her older brother Ptolemy
would also sometimes join in the fun. Of course, Cleo gave in and
let her older siblings win.

Cleopatra was the third oldest child in an unruly household and
family. She was born in 69 BC in what was then known as Alexandria,
Egypt. Her father was Ptolemy XII, a strict and boring man. She had an
older brother named Ptolemy, after her father. It was now the year 59
BC, and Cleo was having another lesson with her tutor Philostratos, from
whom she learned the Greek arts of oration and philosophy. Cleopatra
enjoyed every minute she had during these lessons since she had a
chance to learn about culture, language, philosophy, and the world itself
in general. Which many other mere slaves or other women had not.
Cleopatra knew she was more privileged and luckier in this sense. Cleo
would never take her life for granted, even if she didn't have the best
childhood or upbringing. She would do whatever it took to keep herself
from harm and make sure she would make the best decisions for herself
no matter what. Her older siblings despised her, and her younger sister
adored her older sister Berenice.
Cleo, now at the age of ten, was awaiting another sibling. 'Another
son,' Cleo thought as she had found out that she now had another

brother whom her father also called Ptolemy. Cleo could have cared less as she kept herself concentrated on her lessons.

One year later: In 58 BC, Cleo was eleven years of age, she had managed to learn another few languages and she now possessed the power to speak four in total, which included Greek, Egyptian, Latin, and Arabic. Philostratos commended Cleo on her hard work and always told her to strive to be the best she could possibly be. Sometimes Cleo would ask herself why she worked this hard to impress her father. In fact, she decided whatever she did was for herself and herself only. Cleo, as of recent, was annoyed by her little brother, whom she called Ptolly. He was now one year of age, and she wished that he didn't exist. She knew that it wasn't his fault that he was her brother. But his crying and incessant screaming was quite unnerving and annoying at the same time. Especially since Cleo was practising her Roman numerals. Whenever Cleo was in distress, she would cling to a small carving of the goddess Bastet. The goddess of health and fertility. Bastet had the head of a feline and the body of a woman. For some reason holding this small carving Cleo had supposedly gotten from her mother gave her a calming sensation. That is why Bastet was Cleo's favourite Egyptian god. Cleo looked after this one item as carefully as she could because if she ever lost it, she would literally lose her mind. She never met or didn't remember her mother, but she still didn't want to lose that one thing that had belonged to her mother. In the last two years, Cleo was now better befriended with her younger half-sister Arsinoe, as they would now more often converse about day-to-day things. It seemed that Berenice was now spending most of the time asking her servants whether she was the prettiest woman in Egypt or gossiping about the latest Egyptian fashions.

58 BC, Museum, Alexandria: Cleo was being taught an important lesson about the Egyptian Gods and their stories; some were about Osiris and his goddess Isis or mythical creatures that the Egyptians believed in. One was a creature called Horus, half-bird half-man. Another was called Bastet, who was Cleo's favourite Egyptian god.

She was half-feline (cat), half-woman.
'There is an amazing variation between Gods, different
looking creatures. But each of these creatures also have
their own specific abilities, which can impact society in a
good or bad way,' Philostratos explained.
'Bastet is a good creature, though, or is she not?' Cleo
asked in a naive tone.
'She is known for her ability to heal or symbolically
represent health and fertility. That is what is said in Egyptian
scripture,' Philostratos replied. 'There are many other
Egyptian Gods, but those will be covered in your next
lesson; now it is time for your sister Arsinoe's lesson.'
Cleopatra had now heard and learned enough for one
day; she smiled at Arsinoe as she made her way out of the
Museum. Cleopatra, though, still wanted to know more about the
Egyptian gods, she had learnt about some of them, but she wanted
to know about all of them now. Cleo's curiosity got the better of her.
The Library of Alexandria, Cleo thought; that is where she would
then go. Luckily Cleopatra knew a secret pathway into the library since
no one, unless you were the one in charge (a king or pharaoh) could go
directly into the library. Cleo was only allowed into the library if she had
her teacher/mentor Philostratos with her, the same. Otherwise, she was
not allowed to be unaccompanied anywhere, which meant other than the
Museum or, on occasion, the library she was mostly kept in the safety of
the palace walls. Of course, Cleo didn't care; she snuck around many
corridors until she was in the inner sanctum of the library, which seemed
like it had a ceiling that could pierce and reach the sky. Cleo was
always wowed by what she called the wondrous library. Cleo was
happily scrounging through the old and dusty scrolls as she tried to find
anything interesting to read. *Thud!* Something fell to the ground, it
seemed to be a scroll about the subject Cleo had been trying to find. It
said, "Myths of the Egyptian Gods". Learning the Egyptian language
paid off since Cleo was the only one in her family who could read, write
and speak it. Cleo read the following. It seemed there was also a god
with the head of a dog or jackal called Anubis, who was the
keeper/guardian of the underworld. Another goddess was also depicted,
Sekhmet, who had the head of a lion and a woman's body. Then there
was the sun god Ra, the mighty Ra. Cleo already had heard of this god
in the palace and especially from her father on many occasions. It is
funny to think
that Cleopatra's name in Greek actually meant 'glory of her father';
Cleo always laughed at this thought, since her father never really,
even if barely, noticed her presence. It was now time for Cleo to go
to what she called home, since she could already notice someone's
footsteps moving closer towards her, and of course, she didn't want
to get caught sneaking around in the library.

Back at the Egyptian Palace: Cleo was back in her large room; at least she wasn't alone, as she had her cat by her side.

'Mau come here!' Cleo said. She had brought some food for Mau, which she had snuck from the cooks.

'Meow ... meow,' Mau said in reply and then started purring in Cleo's lap.

Cleo gave Mau some of the delicious fish she had brought with her. It seemed that Mau loved the fish, and as a thank you of sorts, Mau licked Cleo's hands as a sign of affection. Mau ran off and was back up to her old tricks. Cleo was glad that Mau was out of the room because her sister Arsinoe was now in her room. Arsinoe, for some reason, hated cats. Even though most of her family loved felines. Maybe it was because every time she came into contact with them, she would sneeze; that is why Arsinoe probably preferred dogs.

'I know that you went to the library on your own. But I won't tell anyone of your misbehaviour,' Arsinoe said in a cheeky voice.

'Dear little sis, what do you want in exchange for your silence?' Cleo asked.

'I want to learn some Egyptian since you are such an expert in this language,' Arsinoe whispered.

'Why would you want to know? ... Learn Egyptian!' Cleopatra said.

'I want to be able to speak a little because of ...' Arsinoe said.

Cleopatra interrupted, 'A boy; it is always because of a boy.'

'No! No, it is because I want to show Ptolemy, our older brother, that I am better in something than he is!' Arsinoe said.

'Okay, okay, no problem. We have a deal.' Cleo promised to teach Arsinoe a few words so she wouldn't be dobbed in by her.

The next morning Cleo awoke to find Berenice sitting on her bed with a slight frown on her face.

'What have you been up to Cleo? I have seen you and Arsinoe whispering in your room yesterday,' Berenice asked.

'Nothing that concerns you, Berrynice,' Cleo said in a sarcastic tone.

'Awe, as if nothing happened, you are probably pulling off another one of your pranks,' Berenice said.

'What pranks, may I ask, have I ever pulled on you? Since you are always the one to start fights and spread rumours,' Cleo said defiantly.

'Well never mind then ... but before I forget, father has asked for your presence in his throne room,' Berenice said and left the room in a flutter.

Cleo noticed that her sister, for some reason, was jealous of her, but why? Unimportant and confusing thoughts were circling Cleo's mind all at once: What does father want of me now? He has never noticed my presence, yet he now asks me to come to his throne room. Cleo was always the tactical, intelligent, clever, inconspicuous, strategic,

and plainly the most ignored person in the family; that is how she
liked it. It was like she was invisible, but behind the scenes, she could do
whatever she wanted for herself whenever she wanted. Her older brother
Ptolemy XIII was the heir to the throne, and that was his responsibility,
or her other younger brother Ptolemy XIV would take that burden in the
event of the older brother's death. Her oldest sister would probably be
married off to some other king in another foreign land, and the same fate
would be in store for Arsinoe and herself. Women never played a role in
foreign affairs, war or politics. They were merely there to have the
children or play as pawns in the men's games. Cleo didn't want to be just
another mere dumb pawn. She wanted to think, feel, and observe as she
saw fit. But she would always do this in silence since whenever a woman
demonstrated some sort of power, intelligence, or special ability, they
were either punished, exiled, or executed. This was a lot to think about
for an eleven-year-old but Cleo was beyond her age. She acted as if she
was already an adult. In reality, Cleo always tried to act like a
submissive, kind daughter. To the outside world anyway. Cleo made
herself ready and presentable and made her way, through the grand
hallways, down giant stairs until she was in the so-called throne room.
She was now in the presence of her father, Ptolemy XII, who was
wearing his ugly Egyptian head garment as always. The only thing Cleo
liked about that ugly thing was the snake engraving. Cleo waited for her
father to speak, but it seemed like he was waiting for her to say
something first.
'What begs for my appearance, father?' Cleo barely managed to ask.
'We have to leave at once. You and me together!' Ptolemy XII said.
'What about your sons, who are your heirs, and your other daughters?'
Cleo replied with a rather blank expression on her face.
'Of course, your brothers will come with us, but your sisters will
remain in Alexandria for now,' her father said in an annoyed tone.
'Why ... why do you want me to come with you? Why and where
are we leaving?' Cleopatra said in a rushed voice.
'We are leaving soon, and that is that. For reasons you will soon
enough know about, now leave and go back to your room,' Cleo's
father said and banged his sceptre to the ground.
Two guards escorted Cleo back to her room. Cleo steadied her
mind and herself as she was about to embark on a journey somewhere.
She had never left Alexandria before, but she vowed to return to her
home country and birthplace someday. She said her farewells to her
cat Mau and left Alexandria the next day.

58 BC, Europe: It seemed that her father, Ptolemy XII, had been
exiled from Alexandria, leaving Arsinoe and Berenice in Egypt. The
reason for his exile was still unknown to her, but according to her older
brother Ptolemy XIII, he was exiled because he was too dumb to rule his
own country. Weeks later Cleo found out, while she was listening in on

one of her father's conversations with some ambassadors from other countries, that he was exiled because he was bankrupt and owed money to the Roman Empire. For once, her older brother was right. He was an imbecile and a twat. It meant that because of her father, she couldn't return to Egypt unless the Romans allowed her. Months went by like nothing had happened. Cleo and her family were travelling from village to village in the country of Greece, from Rhodes to Athens and then onwards to Italy. Where they stayed in the villa of triumvir Pompey in the Alban Hills, near Praeneste, Italy. They would remain there for a duration of one year. But this one year would be a year Cleo would never forget. When they arrived at this villa, Cleopatra understood her true purpose for her being there. As she could read, write and fluently speak many languages, she would accompany her father on his visits to his so-called alliances, where she would converse with people from many different ethnic backgrounds. She was the translator, the intermediate, and the one who would solve quarrels where there would be none to have had. All her father's advisors adored Cleopatra and her wit. But not all adored her in a good way, as there were other allies there with an even more perverse nature than her father.

A month later, something happened that Cleo never forgot. She was awoken from her sleep and escorted to a room in the villa. For some reason, there was an Egyptian priest there. Cleo knew there was something wrong. She tried to escape, but she couldn't. It was now clear to her that today here in this villa in Italy, she was to marry her own father. Cleo stood facing her father. While the Egyptian priest uttered some Egyptian words. It is not like she would be Queen of Egypt since her father only had wives for more children.
'Nothing bad will happen, Cleo. I am doing this to solidify my rule back in Egypt,' Ptolemy XII said in a calm voice.
Cleo stood there like a twig that had been snapped in half.
As if nothing bad will happen! I, a girl of nearly twelve years, am to marry my own father! What bad luck I have had this past year. I am a pawn in my father's twisted game, Cleo thought to herself. When the ceremony was finally over. Cleo's father let her leave the room. Cleo was disgusted by her father. For now, she still could have her own sleeping quarters but who knew how long that would last? She thought about all the other poor women in her family who committed incest so that the men could maintain a pure Ptolemaic bloodline. That is not what Cleopatra wanted for herself.
A week later her older brother found out about this news and laughed his head off. 'My poor sister Cleo is now the wife of our father! I have heard enough for one day.'
Cleo couldn't take this laughter anymore. She walked toward her brother and struck him on the face. Luckily her brother didn't care, as he continued to laugh as he walked off.

57 BC, Outskirts of Rome, Italy: 'There are rumours circulating that your eldest daughter Berenice has sought to usurp you the rightful King of Egypt and now a loyal spy to our cause has also confirmed that he had seen your daughter in Rome. According to this intel, she was there to see the Roman delegates so that she can gain support for her to become the new Queen of Egypt,' Ptolemy's advisor said in a somewhat unsteady tone. Ptolemy XII replied, 'I wasn't expecting this. We must move forward with our plans at once.'

Ptolemy's adviser rushed out of the villa. Cleo was hiding amongst some shrubs and was asking herself what the commotion was about. A few hours later, that same adviser returned with some old wrinkly Roman man. From what she could make out from their conversation this man was named Aulus Gabinius. He was the Roman governor of Syria. What Cleo's father was about to plan with Garbage Gabinius was not going to end well. This arrangement was supposed to ensure that her father could and would safely return to Egypt unharmed so that he could reclaim his rightful place on the throne. This agreement though also came with a high price in gold. To Cleo, it didn't matter. She only wanted to return home, to a country she grew up in and knew. The thought that she would possibly see her dear cat Mau again made her somewhat happy. Cleo still carried her small carved statue of Bastet around with her wherever she went, as for some strange reason she thought that this gave her a soothing effect on her mind.

55 BC, Alexandria: She was back. Back home where she belonged. Cleo was standing in her old room, which for the last three years had served as someone's study. Cleo ordered a few servants to furnish it with the same furniture that used to be in her room. It took a gruelling two years to get back to Alexandria with the help of Baldinius. No, he was called Gabinius. But now, finally, she was back. Something or someone was missing, though, her dear cat Mau. Cleo looked all around the palace, but she couldn't find her until she saw Arsinoe playing with Mau.
'Mau!' Cleo shouted as she ran towards Arsinoe's room.

'Since when are you fond of cats?' Cleo asked Arsinoe.
Arsinoe answered back, 'Ever since I have been kept in this room most of the time. So, for the last three years I have for most of the time, only had this cat for company. The servants also fed her. What is her favourite food? Fish or not? It doesn't matter, you are finally back; you all are back, and almost everything can return to normal.'
'Since when have you stopped sneezing around cats?' Cleo asked with a smirk on her face.

'I have been couped up here for most of the time, so I may have just gotten used to the smell and the fur,' Arsinoe replied.
Both sisters laughed together as they had not done so in a long time.
Now Arsinoe asked Cleo a daunting question, 'What will happen to Berenice?'
Now it dawned on Cleo that she would now be the older sister for once.
'I don't know. I ... I am not sure.'

In truth, Cleo knew precisely what would happen to Berenice.
She would be executed for her act of treason against her own father.
Cleo didn't know or had ever thought that Berenice was so driven for power. In sad reality, Cleo didn't care about what happened to Berenice, as she was always so harsh, cold, and mean to her.
The now wise fourteen-year-old Cleopatra gave Arsinoe a word of advice: 'Do not follow in the footsteps of women like Berenice, as this will only get you punished or killed. If you seek power, do it in a form that no one notices what your motives are.'

Cleo took Mau and left Arsinoe's room.
The next day Arsinoe saw for herself what happened to her older sister Berenice as Berenice and her supporters were publicly shamed and executed. Now Arsinoe indeed knew what Cleopatra had meant.

52 BC, Alexandria: Cleopatra was now growing into an even more brilliant, conscientious, and confident person and woman. She was now seventeen years of age. She may have been the so-called wife of her father, but he seemed to leave her alone as he had done for the last six years, since she had to marry him. But that now seemed to change. One time at night, someone snuck into her room and wanted to touch her face. But she couldn't make out who that person was.
All she knew was that it was someone in her family. As they wore jewellery only the royals wore. Cleo was uncertain and even frightened at the thought of someone in her family watching her sleep at night.

Cleo had a growing suspicion that this behaviour would continue and escalate into something worse. When she asked her guards who stood outside her bedroom, since this had happened the second time, both would claim not to have seen anyone. Cleo believed they were either loyal to the other person or were bribed to keep their mouths shut. Tonight, Cleo told herself she would spend the night with her sister Arsinoe as she didn't feel safe by herself or in her room for that matter. Arsinoe didn't mind as they would be able to read some old scrolls together. Before both went to sleep, Cleo, as she did every night prayed to the goddess Bastet for health and goodwill. But of all nights, Cleo asked for one more thing, she wished to be kept from harm, or she wished she could have the power to protect herself from harm and to protect other things she cared about. Cleo went to sleep, but what happened next was hard to imagine.

Arsinoe's room: The skies were clear, and one could see the stars. But the night had an eery calmness about it. A slight breeze came to and fro from Arsinoe's room, when in an instant a creature appeared. Cleo awoke to see something she had never thought to encounter in her own lifetime. She saw a creature with a feline's head and a woman's physical body. Cleo couldn't believe her eyes. She thought she was hallucinating. The goddess reached out for Cleo's hand and pulled her up from the bed. For some reason, Arsinoe was in a sort of catatonic state or deep slumber from which she would not wake, not now anyway. Bastet the cat goddess, now took Cleo's other hand and pulled it towards her feline head. Cleo now knew this wasn't a dream. She could feel the fur of Bastet's head, and she could also hear her purring.
'You can now see that I am real or not?' Bastet asked.
'Yes, you are! I ... I believed you existed, but I never thought I would get the honour of meeting a god. My favourite god at that. But what is the reason for you to appear before me?' Cleo replied.
'You asked for my help, so I came to help. I do help other people with their health and all that. But I only reveal myself to people who have the potential to be or become more. Thousand or so years ago, there was a young woman of royal blood just like you. Her name was

Hatshepsut. Every man in the land underestimated her, but with
my help, she grew into Egypt's greatest ruler/pharaoh. She ruled for
some time, she had a daughter, whom she wanted to bestow her gifts.
But she never got the chance because they killed her daughter after
she died and destroyed any trace of her existence. They erased her
from time itself Cleo. You don't want this to happen to you, Cleo,'
Bastet explained.
All Cleo ever wanted for herself was to be able to be who she
wanted to be and now that Bastet came to her, she now knew she
had a further chance at doing so.
'Why me though, what is so special about me?' Cleo asked in a
stern voice.
Cleo was excited to meet the god she idolised ever since she was
a small child. But she still was careful when it came down to it since
she wanted to know what strings were attached to Bastet's appearance
in Arsinoe's room.
'Have you heard of many famous heroines throughout history?
Have you heard of any female conquerors or queens of any countries?
Throughout time women have and will always have to remain in the
men's shadow, hoping that they could one day control their own lives
and destinies. I have chosen you, Cleopatra because you are smart,
charismatic, and have a diplomatic way of doing things. Your position in
Egyptian society also makes you an influence on the common folk. That
is what makes you the perfect person to bestow these gifts/ powers I
have for you. You will be one of the first of a species of cat people,'
Bastet explained in further detail.
'Cat people ... what exactly do you mean by cat people?' Cleopatra
asked.
Bastet yawned for a moment and said, 'You will have the ability
to hear what others cannot, you will be able to see in the dark, you
will have a superior smell and you will be able to transform into a
predator of the night. If you ever stumble or fall, you will always land on
all four or two feet. You will be what Hatshepsut once was and also
could have been. But ...'
'There is a price to all of this power, isn't there?' Cleo asked casually.
'Yes, there is. If you bite or scratch someone, they will also turn
into a cat person. The other thing is that since you are to be the first
of the first cat people of this line, when you die, every thousand or
so years, you will be reincarnated to live amongst the people of this
earth once more. Your people or descendants will call on you for help
or guidance since you will be the first of your kind,' Bastet replied.
'You want me to build or create a race of cat people? My descendants?
What are you talking about?' Cleo asked.
'Dear Cleopatra, it is all for you to decide. Do you wish to be able to
be strong enough to quash any threat that comes your way, or do you
want to cower in the shadows forever? Someday you will decide who

to trust and who you will decide to turn into a feline predator. When it comes to your descendants, someday, you will have children, and each generation will be bestowed with the same power I am offering you now. Take it or leave it, Cleo,' Bastet said in a monotone voice. 'I have decided to accept your offer. I cannot refuse such a proposal. It is an honour to have met you in the first place,' Cleo replied. 'I am glad that you have decided to accept this gift. I hope to see you doing many great things with this power. Now please take my hand,' Bastet said.

Cleo took both hands of Bastet. Shortly afterward, a weird glow emanated from Bastet herself, and this glow or beam of light went into Cleo. As quick as Bastet had come, she was also now gone. Cleo awoke out of the best sleep she had had in ages. She felt like she could smash stone. Now whether she could really do so was another thing. In the next few days, Cleo noticed that her hearing had improved immensely. She could hear the mice and rats fighting over or nibbling at some old rotten food. She could hear servants arguing miles away. She could hear her father in his throne room arguing with his advisors. Her sense of smell also improved, but sometimes she would smell things she didn't want to smell. For instance, rotten food, and her brother, whom she now noticed, stank far worse than she thought before. Cleo also now craved certain foods, like fish, mainly fish, all kinds of fish, grilled or cooked it didn't matter what kind of dish. In truth, Cleo now exhibited all the behaviours of her dearly beloved cat Mau. Mau, on the other hand had taken more of a liking to Arsinoe, ever since Cleo accepted Bastet's gift. Whenever Cleo got too close to Mau, the cat would growl and try to scratch at her. Cleo tried to understand Mau's mindset but left Mau alone with Arsinoe.

On the night after Cleo had been bestowed these grand powers. She would finally manage to find out who had been stalking her when she slept. Cleo decided to sleep in her own room where she awaited the presence of this bastard, the pervert that came at night. This person unknown to her, quietly entered the room, grabbed Cleo by the arms then started caressing her cheek, and then went to kiss her on the lips. Cleo could notice that this person wore the clothes of Egyptian royalty. She tried to push the person away but in trying to do so, for the first time ever, she accidentally transformed into a huge, black-as-night feline predator. The person must have shrunk back and have been startled as they had tried to escape, but before they could do so, Cleo flung the person across the room with her newfound powers and the intruder banged their head against a wall. 'So much for trying to blend in and act normal as a cat person.' Cleo, indeed, now was reaping the benefits of this power. She now had the power to stand up to her enemies and sly, disgusting perpetrators. Cleo thought it was a disgrace to find out her brother was that one person who had tried to take advantage of her. Cleo let her brother lie there for another few hours as it seemed he had been knocked unconscious by the blow to his head. Once he awoke, though, he was rude and obnoxious enough to ask what had happened. Cleo knew that he was acting as if he had forgotten what had happened. So, she played along as she knew that her father would believe any word flowing from her older brother Ptolemy XIII. She also knew that if her brother tried to tell anyone what had happened, no one would believe that he had witnessed his sister turn into a creature that resembled a rather large house-cat like Mau.

'Can you now leave my room?' Cleo asked in a diplomatic tone.

'Only if you want me to, dear sister,' Ptolemy XIII said in a sly manner.

Cleo whispered something into his ear, 'The next time you won't be walking out of here alive, do you understand? You now know what I am capable of.'

Ptolemy's whole facial expression seemed to be collapsing into a pathetic depressed look. He left the room and since then hadn't bothered Cleo in her room. Cleo, of course now had to keep her eyes wide open, even wider open than she had before. She had a pervert brother, or brothers, and a creepy old father to whom she was married.

When Cleo asked Arsinoe whether she was disturbed at night by something, Arsinoe would try to deny anything did happen and tried to shrug it off. Though one could see something was on Arsinoe's mind. Cleo tried or wanted to help her sister but was unsure whether she should do so as her sister was a bit of a gossiper, just like Berenice. Arsinoe was always the informant for Berenice and sometimes even had the ideas for the pranks that Cleo was to suffer from. Who says that even if Cleo helped her sister, that Arsinoe wouldn't, for some reason tell on her. Cleo decided to let Arsinoe fend for herself for now.

Early in the year 51 BC, Ptolemy XII's bed chamber: Death was near for Cleopatra's father. Cleo knew this as she could smell, sense and hear that his body was finally failing him. Why though was another question as her father was always a healthy and weary man. He even had his own servants who had to test his food before he would. So that if they fell ill, then he wouldn't. But this time around, something went horribly wrong. Sinister thoughts were circling Cleo's mind, and now she knew who could have done the deed of killing her father. Cleo could smell some kind of poison or distinct smell on her father's new ring. The one he had received from his eldest son on his birthday. Cleo glared back angrily at her older brother Ptolemy XIII. But he only smirked. Arsinoe stood next to him. It looked like she didn't want to, but Ptolemy held his hand on her shoulder so she couldn't move from her position. Someone entered the room. It was Cleo's other younger brother Ptolemy XIV. He ran to his father, but for some reason, Ptolly's mentor didn't let him go near him. 'Oh! Because he would otherwise come in contact with the poison.' Cleo now knew not to get too close to her father. She wanted to reassure him that he would have a safe journey to the afterlife. But in reality, she really couldn't care less what happened to him. He forced her to marry him. Maybe he was even to blame for these night-time visits she had to endure. But no one should have to suffer at the hands of one's own family. Not even her intrepid father, by his son, that he loved so dearly.

Cleo's father wanted to say something, 'I ... I have something to say,' Ptolemy XII said in a rather husky and croaky voice.

'Do not overstrain yourself,' Cleo said.

But of course, her father persisted. 'I ... my will, here is my will.'

Cleo grabbed the papyrus scroll and put it aside.

'I will make sure that Ptolemy gets it,' she replied.

Ptolemy XII gasped his last breath and was gone. Cleo closed his eyelids and decided she would now go back to her room. She wanted to grasp the scroll when she noticed that it was no longer there as well as her brother Ptolemy. It seemed that in her father's last final moments all Ptolemy could think about was who was to succeed him. Cleo was sure of the fact that her father chose Ptolemy XIII his first son, as his sole heir but what happened the next day was unimaginable, to say the least. Pharaoh's throne room the next day: Ptolemy wanted everyone in his new throne room. He requested that everyone attend his coronation of sorts in the throne room. Everyone should wear their best clothes and jewels. Cleo wore a small kind of tiara, which was adorned with the seeing eye, and a dress embroidered in gold Egyptian hieroglyphs. This dress drooped down and touched the floor. Arsinoe wore a shorter dress but a similar style to that of Cleo's. Arsinoe's hair was slightly braided. While Cleopatra decided to just keep it plain and simple. As Cleo's brown-black hair swept down onto her shoulders one could see that Arsinoe was envious of Cleo. Cleo, of course knew this but she still tried to communicate with her sister. They both made their way to the throne room. Once they were there, they both stood in front of their brother with a bunch of other faces some Cleo had never seen before.

'I herewith announce that I am the sole ruler of the Egyptian kingdom as it is stated in this will,' Ptolemy XIII proclaimed.

To Cleo though, it sounded like he wasn't sure of himself in this matter.

Then another man with a large build and a typical Roman outfit said, 'That is not entirely true though, your father also sent me a duplicate copy of his will and it states that you are not the only heir of his Egyptian Kingdom,' Gabinius said.

'Probably Ptolly is the second Egyptian heir!' Cleo thought to herself.

'Well, who do you claim shares this honour?!' Ptolemy XIII said in a confused tone.

'Cleopatra VII Philopator is to be a joint ruler with you Ptolemy XIII,' Gabinius said in an annoyed tone.

Ptolemy XIII frowned. 'This cannot be possible, as I possess the right will. Right here in front of me,' Ptolemy shouted.

'I would make no such accusations if they were not true. So that will you possess must have been forged by someone,' Gabinius argued. 'May I also add, that your father made Cleopatra his regent in the event of his death. Your father told me this about a year or so ago,' Gabinius said.

'Isn't it true that you were put on trial for betraying the Roman Empire Gabinius?' Ptolemy replied.

'Yes, that is, but your father was a true friend to me and he was true to his word. Which I can't say the same for you. As for my indiscretions, they have nothing to do with the fact that your sister, who is standing here before you now is also a ruler of Egypt. I just want to fulfill your father's last wish.'

Gabinius gave the papyrus scroll to some other Egyptian officials, who also confirmed that Cleo was to be a joint ruler with her brother and that the scroll that Gabinius possessed was authentic. All this meant to Cleo was that she would have to now marry her brother, as this was Ptolemaic tradition.

'Couldn't Arsinoe have been joint ruler with her brother?' Cleo questioned herself. As always, it was now Cleo's turn to be in the limelight with her co-ruler brother Ptolemy XIII.

Cleo didn't want to have this new responsibility. She would rather have continued to stay in the shadows and watch other idiots fighting over unimportant things. Now she had no choice in this matter, and there wouldn't be any way for her to get out of this now. This joint rule wouldn't last long as both siblings especially Ptolemy were planning their own plots to overthrow one another. They both would now inherit the debt their father had accumulated over a long time. That is why he probably chose Cleo as one of his heirs, since she probably was one of the only people smart enough to handle and deal with the debt collectors.

50 BC, Alexandria (named after Alexander the Great), Egypt:
An array of many things had happened during the course of one year. Cleopatra now had the public's support more than her brother had. Cleo may have been feared by some or others were wary of her, but she was otherwise adored by Egypt's people. At the start of her new reign, she erected many statues in honour of many Egyptian gods.

Cleo also faced several high-stakes issues and emergencies shortly after taking the throne, these included famine caused by drought and a low level of the annual flooding of the Nile river. But after she had managed to help the people of Egypt through these tough times, the people thought that she was one of the best rulers that they had, had in a long time. Cleo, in this rather short time had brought more peace and solidarity to her rule and her country. The people may have been suspicious and careful of Cleopatra their new queen at the start since she had also miraculously combatted many problems in her first year of rule. But the public's applause for Cleopatra outweighed those who were weary of her. Some of Alexandria's people even thought Cleo was some sort of witch or god since Cleo sometimes dressed up like the goddess Isis at some of the Egyptian festivals she attended.

Cleo was grateful or hoped that they didn't think she was a bad witch. Ptolemy XIII, on the other hand was busy making deals that were of the heinous kind. As he was planning to overthrow his sister Cleo.

Ptolemy XIII was never interested in the people or the country itself, he was interested in war, politics, and gaining new territories. Cleo knew that something was going to happen. She noticed that Ptolemy also wasn't in the throne room as often as he had been in the past. With her extreme senses, she could overhear her brother talking of plans to either assassinate or overthrow her. Cleo had to tell Charmion this new awful news. Charmion was one of Cleo's servants. Over this one year, Cleo and Charmion had become good friends. They were, in fact such good friends that they even became their own confidants. Cleo trusted Charmion that she confided every secret, even that of her powers. But that was only ever since Charmion saved Cleo's life.

In 51 BC, there was an Egyptian Banquet held and Cleo almost ate something that could have killed her. Cleo didn't know that her brother had poisoned the one thing that she had liked eating the most, fish. That if eaten in small amounts it wouldn't be detected only making the person slightly ill. But if consumed in large amounts the person meets a fatal end. Charmion stopped Cleo from eating the fish that had been marinated in some kind of sauce. She told Cleo that she had been ordered by Ptolemy to marinate the fish with some kind of poisonous properties and that she had no choice in doing so. As Ptolemy had threatened her own life. Charmion though it seemed, had a conscience, a benevolent one at that. From then onwards their friendship blossomed and Charmion was under Cleo's protection. Cleo was not only befriended with Charmion but also with a woman named Eiras. Eiras was rejected by her own family because she was different. Eiras was born with a deficiency that affected her bones, thus making her useless. But to Cleo, she was a dear friend. Ptolemy found her as a joke because of her ailment, and gave her as a present to Cleo to be a servant, so he could again ridicule his sister. That is how Eiras came to Cleo. Cleo didn't try to judge anyone based on their appearance or intellect.
Cleo always told this to her closest confidants, 'I accept others, as long as others accept me.'
With this Eiras and Charmion agreed. One night Cleo had a dream as to how she could indirectly heal Eiras. She remembered the night so long ago where she met Bastet. Bastet had mentioned one important thing, that if she scratched or bit someone else, they would be like her. Maybe this would help Eiras? Maybe she could then be normal just like everyone else? Cleo asked herself. Cleo had thought about all this the year before, and now she was losing time. Her dear friend Eiras had fallen to the ground and for some reason was struggling to breathe. Cleo ordered Egyptian physicians/healers to tend to her wounds and to tell her what was wrong with Eiras. They told her there was nothing they could do as she had a collapsed organ or lung. Cleopatra now knew Eiras's

end was near, but she couldn't bear the thought of losing one of the only people that truly understood her. It is now or never, Cleo told herself. If she didn't try this now, then she would lose her forever. Cleo grasped Eiras's hand. She looked into Eiras's dark brown eyes.

In a quiet tone, Cleo said the following: 'You know what I am. You can also be like me. That is if you want to be like me. This is a choice for you to make. Just know that I will support you the whole way.'

'I have always been a fragile mess. Haven't I?' Eiras managed to utter.

'Yes, you have, but I will not let you die if you don't have to,' Cleo replied.

'Then please do it now,' Eiras said.

Cleo transformed her hand into a feline paw and used one of her claws to scratch Eiras's hand. Charmion stood guard by the door as she made sure that no one saw what happened next. Eiras who was lying on Cleo's bed began to jolt back and forth in an aggressive sort of movement. Eiras began to scream out in pain as she also tried to lunge at Cleo and Charmion. Cleo put a piece of cloth which was wrapped around a piece of wood in Eiras's mouth as a way of calming her down and keeping her quiet at the same time. Charmion tried to strap her down, but it wouldn't hold. Cleo hoped that this transformation wouldn't be so painful for her friends. But now she knew the toll it took on them as she witnessed her friend tossing and turning and tumbling to the floor multiple times. In the morning though Eiras looked like a changed person.

When Cleo asked how Eiras felt she would reply with, 'I believe this transformation has given me my life back. The life I never had. I always felt like I would break into tiny pieces before but now I feel like I could smash something ... anything. Last night my insides felt like they were being crunched and moving back into place. The pain was worth it.'

'What can you do? Do you have improved senses as Cleo has?' Charmion asked out of curiosity.

'I can hear the insects eating away at a carcass miles away. I can hear children playing outside. I can smell your hair. It smells atrocious. I can hear and smell things I haven't ever noticed before,' Eiras replied.

'I will teach you what it means to be what I am, a cat person. You will control your urge to hunt or lunge at everything that annoys you. You will learn the ability to transform at will into a feline of the night. Anything and everything is open to you Eiras,' Cleo explained.

All three laughed at one another, but this moment of happiness wouldn't last long.

49 BC, Alexandria, Egypt: It was a day like any other for Cleo. She

would pretend to be an obedient wife and co-ruler with her brother Ptolemy XIII. But that was all a guise so she would have time to plan for a strategy to overthrow her brother. Her brother as of recent, had started signing royal documents with his name before hers. Which showed that he was planning something very soon. When he was planning to overthrow Cleo was the question. Now that Cleo was Queen of Egypt she also had access to the Library of Alexandria whenever she wanted. That secret passageway she had found or used as a little girl she now used at night, to get to the library undisturbed. Cleo with her friends, was trying to find a way to overthrow Ptolemy so that he would never have the same chance to do so with her. But finding any evidence of infidelity or any evidence of wrongdoing was hard to find. On one of these nights, however, Charmion found an old book which went into the family history of the Ptolemaic dynasty. It stated what Cleo already knew for a fact that she and her family were descended from a Greek general named Ptolemy I 'Soter', a general and friend of Alexander the Great. Something on the page though caught Cleo's attention, it stated that after Berenice had been born, there was another child her older brother Ptolemy, but it seemed like his name was stuck over where someone else's should have been. Cleo and Charmion carefully removed the piece of paper that was stuck over the other name. What they saw next caught them by surprise. The name that was under Ptolemy was Ptolemaia. It seemed Cleo should have had an older sister and not a brother. Next to the name though, was some sort of symbol, which Cleo later found out meant stillborn. Her sister never was alive, it seems she was replaced by someone with another baby Cleo came to know as her older brother Ptolemy XIII. Lies upon lies. Conspiracies upon conspiracies. Who swapped the infants? Who would stand to gain from this? All these thoughts were swirling in Cleo's mind all at once. Until Cleo came to the conclusion that Ptolemy XIII may not be her brother but her cousin and that he could have been swapped at birth, so that her father believed he had gotten a son. But in reality, her father's brother wanted to ensure that his son would end up on the Egyptian throne. What a Ptolemaic conspiracy that would be? Cleo asked herself. The only reason Cleo thought the infants were
swapped by one of her uncles was because they both envied their brother, who had received the Egyptian territory. One of her uncles especially, when Cleo was younger, had shown an immense amount of interest in anything and everything Ptolemy did.
'Enough for today,' Cleo told her friends/accomplices. Assumptions at the end of the day do not make what Cleo found true. At least Cleo now knew that her brother wasn't her true brother. Eiras and Charmion took the book with them to Cleo's room. In the next few days, Cleo would unravel the mysteries that surrounded her family lineage.

Somewhere in Alexandria 49 BC: She had to flee, and she had no choice. Cleo had to leave the palace as she was almost killed by someone who was ordered to kill her. Cleo had only managed to gather a few things. She wasn't even able to rescue her friend Charmion from her fake older brother Ptolemy's grasp. Arsinoe, Eiras, and a few others managed to help Cleo. Cleo had to think fast. Where could she go and seek refuge so she could regain her strength. Cleo decided to stay with one of the delegates in Alexandria who always supported her decisions. Once Cleo was in a safer place, she now had to think of a strategy so that she could then regain her rightful position as the Pharaoh of Egypt. Before Cleo had to escape from the city she was about to reveal or expose the truth about Ptolemy's true lineage and that he was in fact, the son of her uncle Ptolemy of Cyprus. But Cleo never had the chance to reveal the truth since she was forced from the palace. It was as if Ptolemy knew exactly what Cleo had planned to do. Maybe he had his own spies watching her every move. Now it didn't matter. Cleo now had to think about how she would regain the power she had lost. She may not have wanted this power in the past, but now that she had lost it, she wanted it back. Cleo never thought that she would want to be queen or pharaoh of a country now though she craved being in command again. With the help of Eiras her servant, Cleo gathered help from her many faithful supporters in Alexandria and waged war against her brother, who wanted to keep his precious power. Cleo didn't have a choice, she would have kept on the joint rule with Ptolemy but it was now certain to her that Ptolemy wanted all the power to himself. Another thing Cleo had found out just before she left her own home, was the fact that her sister Berenice didn't betray her father willingly. She was forced by her own father, Ptolemy XII to commit treason. She had found an old papyrus scroll in the library which was sent to Berenice ordering her to take it upon herself to be

the queen of Egypt as sole ruler. Cleo felt sorry for Berenice in this one instance as it wasn't her fault that she had to follow her father's orders. Cleo's own father must have wanted Berenice out of the way for some reason. When Cleo wanted to put the papyrus scroll away, another piece of papyrus that was, for some reason wedged in the other one fell to the ground. Cleo picked up the piece of papyrus and she could recognise Berenice's handwriting in Latin on the paper. Good fortune was on Cleo's side since she was able to read Latin. Cleo didn't know though, that Berenice could understand yet even write Latin as well. It seems that Cleo underestimated her own sister's capacity to learn.

Cleo read the following (translated from Latin):

27

To whomever finds this letter,
It has recently come to my attention that my uncle is the true
father of who I thought was my brother Ptolemy XIII. This
revelation made me utmost uneasy. I also want to state that
I Berenice never chose to betray Egypt, yet its rightful ruler
Ptolemy XII. For some reason, I have been forced to make
these decisions. I have never told this anyone, if anyone from
my family reads this piece of scrap, when I was younger, I
witnessed an awful thing. Ptolemy XIII at night murdered my
infant brother Ptolemy XIV. The poor baby was smothered
to death. I hid behind a wall and let my brother commit this
atrocity. After this happened my father Ptolemy XII, kept
a close eye on the next infant that was born and also named
him Ptolemy XIV. I never wanted to be queen; I never had
this kind of ambition. The actions I will now take were never
my own decision. If you ... if anyone is reading this letter. I
will soon ... I will already be dead. This is for my sisters
please be wary of this phrase 'socius et amicus populi Romani.'
Berenice IV
Daughter of Ptolemy XII
Pharaoh of Egypt

What did Berenice mean with that phrase 'friend and ally of the Roman people'? Cleo told herself that she would probably someday soon find out herself what Berenice meant. Arsinoe remained by Cleo's side the whole way. She was like a loyal cat or dog. Which seemed out of the ordinary for her since she never was interested in anything Cleo had to say. Eiras decided to keep an eye on Arsinoe of her own volition. Cleo also had her suspicions about Arsinoe, but she still hoped that Arsinoe only had good intentions for her for presence here with her. Weeks now went by as if they almost flourished into one big blur. Cleo felt hopeless. She felt like she was smashing her head against a never-ending wall that wouldn't break down. Whenever Cleo felt like she was making progress it was the opposite. It was another push-back. For the last few weeks and then months Cleo was fighting back against her brother, and now she had no choice but to flee from Alexandria itself for good. Cleo now planned to travel towards the region of Thebes so she could come up with a strategic plan. After she had agreed to one last joint decision with her brother to give Pompey military aid. She had no choice afterward but to leave immediately. When they arrived in Thebes, Cleo started devising a plan which she kept to herself. They would spend many weeks there.

48 BC, spring, continent of Africa: Arsinoe was growing tired of travelling because after spending another few weeks in Thebes they would travel towards the Roman-controlled Syria. Where Cleo

planned to gather an invasion force that would then head towards Egypt. Eiras followed Cleo's each and every step. Making sure that she would not stumble or fall. As Cleo, Arsinoe, Eiras, and their Syrian army made their long way back to Egypt. A few days later, in the distance, Cleo could make out the pyramids, and she knew that she was almost back home. Cleo decided to stay away from the busy Egyptian centre. Since she didn't want to bring any attention to herself and her forces. When night fell Cleo decided to check out the perimeter. Of course, she wouldn't be doing this in her human form. Felines can see at night-time since they are also nocturnal predators. Cleo transformed into her cat form. She now was as black-as-night and she could blend into the dark of the night. Cleo felt like she was being watched. She could hear footsteps from afar. It only was Eiras who was also in her cat form.

Eiras wanted to help Cleo so both of them disappeared into the darkness. They both pounced on buildings and used their keen sense of smell, sight, and sound. Cleo and Eiras now stood in close vicinity to the royal palace. But armed men stood in their way. Not just a few men, but a whole army stood guard. Holding their spears as tightly as possible. Luckily Cleo and Eiras were hidden behind a statue. They both decided to retreat to their base. Cleo knew that it would be impossible to invade Alexandria with the lack of resources she possessed. So, she only had one last thing she could do. She would now seek assistance from Rome. From Julius Caesar to be exact. Cleo, though, was unaware that her sister Arsinoe had just witnessed her transforming from a large cat predator into her normal human self. Arsinoe didn't know whether she was hallucinating, she decided to go back to sleep and tried to dismiss what she had seen as a dream.

48 BC, Egypt, Nile River: It had been a week since Cleo had sent emissaries to Rome to seek assistance from Caesar and still had received no word from him. Cleo was cooling off herself in the Nile river as it had been a long hot day. When Cleo returned to her sleeping quarters, she saw Arsinoe sitting on the ground. Arsinoe motioned for Cleo to sit down next to her. Arsinoe had something on her mind and Cleo knew this. Arsinoe sat next to Cleo, and she was about to tell Cleo something she had overheard some of the men in their encampment talk about.
Arsinoe began to explain, 'Yesterday I overheard a group of men talking about Caesar and his many mistresses. They were joking that Caesar always preferred the company of his many mistresses to his big-nosed and big-chinned wife Calpurnia.'
'What is the point of our conversation now, dear sister?' Cleo asked

hesitantly.

'Well, since you have not received word back from Caesar, why don't you yourself appear before him and ask for his help. You aren't an unattractive woman. You don't have to have any interactions of an intimate kind, if you know what I mean,' Arsinoe replied.

Arsinoe was right in some respects; maybe Caesar's addiction to women could help Cleo to her advantage. But Cleo didn't want to have to do anything more than use flirtatious behaviour and gestures to persuade a powerful man to regain her power of Egypt. Arsinoe looked at Cleo with a puzzling expression.

'What is on your mind, Cleo?' Arsinoe asked.

Cleo felt a wave of insecurity overcome her and so she replied, 'Thank you for your insights but now I must ask you to leave my humble makeshift room.'

Arsinoe left Cleo alone to contemplate on what steps she might have to take next. Cleo decided to travel towards Rome the next day. However, how she would persuade Caesar to help her was another question.

47 BC, Rome: A lot had happened during the duration of one year. For one, Cleopatra was expecting her first child. As one can guess Cleopatra indeed didn't particularly want to become Caesar's mistress but there was one difference. She was the only one she knew of to give the childless Caesar an heir. Cleopatra had just received word that Egypt had now been liberated of Ptolemy XIII and that he now had been defeated. Funnily enough, Ptolemy drowned during the battle of the Nile while he was trying to escape by boat. Cleo smirked and now looked out at the view of Rome she had while she was standing on her own balcony. All Cleo remembered from a year ago seemed like a distant memory. Cleo arrived in Rome with her sister Arsinoe a year ago and using her charm and wit she won over Caesar quicker than she thought she would. Cleo arrived in her Egyptian clothing and her tiara she wore so elegantly. All the Roman people thought that she was an interesting spectacle to bear witness to, since the public never often saw people dressed like her and her sister. Caesar agreed to give Cleo an army so she could overthrow her brother Ptolemy XIII. But there was a price of course, Cleo would have to become one of Caesar's mistresses. Luckily Cleo managed a way so that she didn't have to have many intimate relations with him. One of these intimate nights though was enough for poor Cleo to end up pregnant. Cleo wanted to terminate the pregnancy once she found out about the foetus, for some reason, Eiras and Arsinoe persuaded her to not harm the baby. The only reason she let it live was because she thought that she needed an heir once Ptolemy no longer was on the throne. During the few months Cleo had spent in Rome, Arsinoe one night spotted Cleo having a nightmare but there was one odd thing about what she witnessed Cleo doing. Cleo was

partially transforming whilst asleep. Arsinoe now knew that what she had seen back in Egypt wasn't a figment of her mind. She definitely now knew that Cleo was some other kind of being. A few days later after Cleo had that awful night terror, Arsinoe began to question what Cleo was. One day and out of nowhere while Cleo was having breakfast, Arsinoe showed Cleo a pillow that had been torn to shreds but still had claw marks on it.

'What kind of creature would do this?' Arsinoe asked in a curious voice.

Cleo failed to respond quickly enough so Arsinoe stormed off.

Later that day, Cleo went to Arsinoe's room. Arsinoe was sitting on her bed looking out the window at the colosseum. Cleo wasn't sure what her younger sister wanted from her, but she felt like she was being pressured into yet another thing she didn't want to do. Cleo went towards Arsinoe and sat down on the other side of the bed.

'What do you want from me, Arsinoe?' Cleo asked casually.

'I want to be what you are so I can defend myself against my enemies,' Arsinoe said angrily.

'I do not know what you are talking about,' Cleo replied.

'Do not deny that you know what I am talking about. Should I show you this pillow to remind you of the obvious?' Arsinoe shouted.

'Yes, I am different, but I cannot give you what you want,' Cleo said.

'Why, why don't you understand!' Arsinoe started to sob.

'I do understand your concerns. I just simply do not trust you. You pressure me into situations. You pretend to want to accompany me. But all you want is power all for yourself!' Cleo justified herself.

'As if you don't want power,' Arsinoe said.

Cleo didn't know how to answer that question and she didn't want to answer that question, so she left the room. A few days later, Cleo found out that Arsinoe had left for Egypt. That is all that had happened over the duration of one year.

Cleo was now sitting on her bed in her own room in Rome. Since Arsinoe left, Cleo was ordered to stay hidden from the public's view as she wasn't supposed to be seen in close proximity to Caesar, since he was married to a rather wealthy Roman woman Calpurnia. Eiras most of the time tried to keep Cleo entertained as she was constantly penned up in her room. On the 23 June 47 BC, Cleo's son Caesarion was born. Cleo didn't want a son; she would have preferred a daughter. Cleo knew though, that Caesar would be overjoyed by the glorious news of his new son. All Cleo now thought about was how to persuade Caesar to let her return to Egypt. Now that she had successfully borne him a son, which most men want, she hopefully would have some leverage in that matter. The following day Cleo thought she had seen a ghost. As

Cleo was preparing for her journey back to Egypt, someone was standing behind her. A servant had brought a dear old friend to her. It was Charmion. The one friend she was not able to take with her from Egypt. Cleo thought about Charmion every day and now that Charmion stood before her, she couldn't believe it. Cleo hugged Charmion. Cleo was overwhelmed with emotions, but she was mostly annoyed with herself that she wasn't able to take Charmion with her. Cleo told herself she wouldn't let Charmion down again let alone out of her sight.

Charmion said, 'It is good to see an old friend. I know you wanted to take me with you, and I am not mad with you for not doing so as you would have probably only endangered yourself.'

'I am so glad to see you. I ... apologise for not coming back for you quick enough.' Cleo almost started to cry.

'It is alright Cleo. I am just happy to be in the company of friends again. At least Ptolemy your older brother won't be bothering us anymore,' Charmion reassured Cleo.

With that statement, both agreed.

'You know how Ptolemy died right?' Charmion asked.

'Yes, he tragically drowned,' Cleo replied.

'That is partially true, and I held him underwater. You see, we were both trying to escape the siege and I had enough of playing his games, so I murdered him,' Charmion said.

Cleo did not care what happened to Ptolemy, but she still didn't think that Charmion was capable of doing such a thing. She was proud of Charmion either way.

A few hours later when Cleo was about to leave Rome, she was blocked by some Roman guards. They told Cleo that on the order of Caesar, she and her son were not to leave Rome. Cleo was kept in her room for many hours while cradling her crying newborn in her arm. Cleo was worried that she would never see Egypt again when another Roman man dressed in their typical clothes came in. This man, however had a higher rank. She knew this man, he was acquainted with Caesar when she arrived in Rome.

His name was ... Mark Antony.

'I am sorry for the delay. I have managed to give you safe passage out of Rome. If that is what you want,' Antony said.

Cleo let Charmion do the talking, as she wasn't in the right state of mind to do so.

Charmion spoke for Cleo, 'Thank you for your kindness. But we have nothing to give or pay you.'

'Nothing would honour me more than helping the beautiful Queen of Egypt,' Antony said.

Cleo thought that this man must have been out of his mind. Beautiful? As if no strings were attached for his help. Cleo didn't want to take this help for granted, so she left for Egypt as quickly as she could.

44 BC, Egypt: The Egyptian throne room looked more magnificent than ever, glistening in the warm sun. Cleopatra had now been the rightful ruler of Egypt for almost three years. For a duration of three quiet years, Cleo had a prosperous and peaceful rule. When she had gotten back from Rome in 47 BC, she found out that she had to again co-rule with her other younger brother Ptolemy XIV whom she also had to marry. It seemed that there was no other choice for women than to rule alongside men. That is what Berenice meant by that phrase, which Caesar loved saying. She only found out that she was a bargaining chip for having a good time, just like Berenice was. The phrase should rather state friends of imbeciles than friends or allies of Rome. Cleo decided to rule with Ptolemy XIV for as long as it would be possible to do so. This co-rule though spooked Cleo because she was awaiting the next plot from her brother to remove her as co-ruler. Cleo's son Caesarion would be turning three years of age this year. Cleo sat on her grand throne and was reminiscing about the past, for instance, when she found out that Arsinoe had worked with her older brother Ptolemy in the siege of Egypt. Arsinoe was afterward paraded through Rome's streets and then exiled to the Temple of Artemis at Ephesus. This all happened right before Cleo had left for Egypt. Cleo was shaken by someone.

It was Charmion. 'Your highness it is time for your midday nap. Come with me.'

Cleo was escorted by Charmion back to her room. For some reason, Cleo felt like someone was closing curtains in front of her eyelids.
'Have you heard back from Rome?' Cleo asked.
'No, we have not received word back yet from Rome,' Charmion replied.
'Charmion would you please go overhear what Ptolemy is talking about with his advisors?' Cleo kindly asked.
'Yes, I will,' Charmion said.
Ever since Cleo was back together with Charmion, she offered her the feline power. Charmion happily agreed and now also had the same abilities as Cleo and Eiras. Cleo fell into a deep sleep from which she would awake much later on.

Someone tried to wake up Cleo. It was Charmion, who had just found out something that Cleo wouldn't want to hear. It took some time for Cleo to shake off the tiredness and when she heard the terrible news, she wasn't able to hold her temper. Cleo started to ball her hands into fists and in a fit of rage, she wanted to give Ptolly a present he would never forget. But Eiras and Charmion got her to calm down so that she would think of this situation more logically and diplomatically. Ptolemy XIV Cleo's younger brother was planning to overthrow his sister just like Cleo's older adopted brother had done. Cleo had to act now if she wanted to take this matter into her own hands. It had taken Ptolemy XIV three years to come up with a plan to overthrow his own sister. Cleo decided she would again travel to Rome like she had done two years ago in 46 BC. In 46 BC though, she only went to Rome because Caesar wanted to see his one and only son, but Cleo also grew fond of Caesar. Cleo's and Caesar's relationship blossomed into something more than just a matter of convenience. On that same visit, Cleo also met Mark Antony again. For some reason, Cleo still remembered the man's name. It didn't matter now, Cleo wanted to see her son Caesarion on the throne after herself and so Cleo began plans to travel to Rome.

44 BC, Rome: Cleo was now back where she had last been about two years ago. Because she had received no response from Caesar, she decided she would travel to Rome herself and greet him personally. He probably will be elated to see Caesarion, Cleo told herself. When Cleo had arrived at Caesar's residence/palace, Cleo asked the servants for Caesar's presence, but none were able to answer her requests. Cleo decided to take up residence in Caesar's villa where she waited for a day.

The next day Caesar, accompanied by Mark Antony, came to greet his son. Caesar though couldn't stay for long as he had other tasks to attend to. He told Cleo that he would see them later that night. Unfortunately, poor Caesar did not know that this would be the last time he would see Cleo and his son alive. Mark Antony decided to keep Cleo and Caesarion company. He would talk with Cleo about the many wars and military campaigns he had fought and how he always would remain loyal to Caesar and Cleo. Cleo noticed that this was turning into an awkward conversation and when she decided she would now go to bed, Antony leaned in and tried kissing Cleo. Cleo leaned backward and then gave Antony an annoyed glare. She called on Caesarion and her servants and decided to go indoors. Antony decided to leave Cleo alone and he would now join Caesar in these boring talks they would always have where they would argue about territories, legislation, new statues, religion, wars, or any incoming threats against Caesar. As of recent tensions in the Roman senate had been growing, but for Antony, these tensions would come and go from time to time, and so he didn't notice the threat that now Caesar's life was in danger. It all happened so fast. Many conspirators from the senate lunged themselves on Caesar all with daggers in their hands. Antony wanted to help Caesar, but he was stopped by other senators from doing so. Caesar was now gone, and Antony was told by the senate that they had no choice and that Octavian according to

Caesar's will was now in charge. Antony left the building at a hastened pace. He couldn't risk that Caesar's child would also be murdered by these men and he also couldn't risk that they would take Cleo hostage. Cleo was in Caesar's villa watching Caesarion play a game with Eiras and Charmion when someone knocked on the door. Cleo asked Eiras to see who it was. Eiras was pushed back by Antony, who had a nervous look in his eyes.

'You must leave now while you still can. Something awful has happened. I will explain later. Make haste. Let us waste no time, as time is of the essence,' Antony said in a rushed voice.

Cleo didn't understand what was wrong. But as she would find out later, what had happened would put her son's life in danger.

44 BC, Egypt: Cleo had arrived back from an arduous journey she had to endure to ensure that she would make it home. Cleo feared for her own and her son's life. She wasn't sure what she would now do at all. She had a brother who planned to depose her and there was a new Roman ruler, Octavian, who was the nephew of Julius Caesar who definitely wasn't an ally of Cleo. The next few steps Cleo would take would decide the fate for herself, her friends, allies, and her only child Caesarion.

44 BC, Egyptian palace, a few months later: Crowds of people were in front of the Egyptian palace celebrating a festival of sorts. Everyone was in a rather cheerful mood, even Eiras and Charmion. Caesarion though wished to play with the other children he had seen outside, but for a boy of now four years anything and everything would seem interesting. Cleo could notice that Caesarion began tapping into his own abilities. He could understand every single word she would ever speak behind thick walls, and he could smell things other people couldn't. That was one of the first few signs. At least Caesarion still hadn't utilised his power to turn into a ferocious feline, as he would probably be a very intolerant one at that. Cleo was now speaking to another few delegates when she decided to leave the throne room and head towards the Library of Alexandria where she would look for some interesting learning material she would instruct Caesarion's tutors to teach him. She wanted her son to learn the things she had learned from her own tutor Philostratos when she herself was young. Cleo wanted her only child to be interested in the marvels of the world, the mystical aspects of the Egyptian culture, and that he would be able to immerse himself in different languages and cultures. She wanted her son to also learn the art of diplomacy, the sciences, philosophy, work on his oratory skills, and of course, mathematics. Caesarion should also be able to ask questions about why or how things work a specific way, Cleo told herself. When Cleo had found the materials or scrolls she wanted her son to learn about, she went back to the palace and wanted to spend some time with

Caesarion who was playing with some sort of toy.

A few hours later it was night-time and Cleo could see it would be a windy night. She could notice that there was going to be a sandstorm, which as Cleo had thought was confirmed the next day, as the whole city of Alexandria was blanketed in a rather thick sand plume. Almost all of Cleo's subjects had problems breathing, even her brother Ptolemy XIV. For some reason Eiras, Charmion, Caesarion, and Cleo were unaffected. Cleo knew why she was not affected by the dust/sand. Rumours though were circulating in the Egyptian palace that Cleo was a witch or mage of sorts and that she put a spell on herself, her closest friends, and her own son and cursed others to suffer from the sandstorm. Cleo knew exactly where this rumour had originated from. As always Cleo would again be bullied and threatened by her own family. Ptolemy XIV always knew that the general public preferred Cleo than they did him and so he decided it was time to get rid of Cleo. What wouldn't be better than to blame a natural occurrence in weather on his own sister, so that all of Egypt's people would also begin to believe the same? Cleo grew more worried each and every day. She knew that trouble was brewing, but she didn't want to have to again do something she didn't want to do.

Charmion could notice that something was troubling Cleo. She asked her queen what was wrong, but she would get no answer. Charmion unfortunately didn't possess the ability to read minds, until one day she overheard a conversation Cleo had with her son Caesarion. 'Mommy is very worried. Hopefully, your uncle isn't going to have to go away. But that decision I leave to him. Whoever makes the first move.'

Charmion hid behind the wall, she now knew what the problem was and there was one thing she could do for Cleo. This one thing though meant she would have to acquaint herself with one of her old suppliers. Charmion knew someone in Alexandria who secretly sold all different kinds of trinkets, hallucinogens, and poisons. Charmion only knew this as a fact because she was ordered by Ptolemy the impersonator king to kill Cleo with a poison. Charmion threatened to tell on the seller if he dared not give her the goods for free, to which the seller agreed. Charmion put a poison called Aconite into her woven bag and went back to the Egyptian palace. Charmion then went to the food preparation rooms where she put some of the poison into a jug of beer that Ptolemy XIV was to drink from. She carried the jug out towards Ptolemy, but she carefully made sure to also bring a cup for herself to drink from which contained no poison, so that if Ptolemy insisted for her to also drink, she would drink from the cup she had prepared beforehand. Cleo sat at the long dining table and stared at Charmion with a confused expression.

Charmion continued to calmly walk towards Ptolemy. She handed him a cup when he asked for her to try some of the beer first. Cleo wanted to get up from her chair, but she knew she would only incriminate herself if she tried to stop Charmion from doing what she was about to do. Cleo's hands were shaking under the table, and sweat was dripping down her face because she was so stressed that Charmion would bring herself into some kind of danger, but there was nothing she could do other than sit and watch. Ptolemy waited for Charmion to take the first sip from her cup. Charmion had her own cup at hand. She drank a large portion and to Ptolemy then it seemed that the beer was fine. Of course, after he had consumed the alcohol, he succumbed to some sort of sickness. He went to his room, where he was found dead the next day. Cleo knew exactly who was responsible. She was glad and thankful. But at the same time, she felt like she had been betrayed by Charmion. Charmion insisted that everything she did was in the best interest of Cleo and Caesarion and that she would do it again if she had the chance. Cleo was unable to understand why Charmion would risk herself for her. It was now evident that Charmion was a true friend who would never let Cleo down.

42 BC, Alexandria, Egypt: As of late, Cleopatra was now sole ruler of Egypt or somewhat sole ruler, as she also appointed her son Caesarion as her co-ruler. Cleo sometimes remembered back to when she was a naive little girl. Maybe not naive, but she dreamt that someday she would be able to do what she wanted when she wanted. She only wanted to fade into the background and let the grown-ups make the decisions. When she was older, she came to understand that she was a pawn in her own father's game and that her brothers fooled her again and again. She even was played by the famous Julius Caesar who was assassinated two years ago. The only man she came to rely on somewhat was Mark Antony, who in the last few weeks had been requesting Cleo's presence in a place named Tarsos. Cleo rejected his offers time and time again, until there was a reason to agree to his offer. Cleo during this meeting had a chance to clear her name for some strategical and tactical mess she was in because of some war.

Cleo decided to sail up the Kydnos River to Tarsos in Thalamegos, somewhere in Anatolia (Turkey). She used her favourite Egyptian ship, which was a large, magnificent, and elegant boat. When Antony saw the ship, he at first couldn't believe his eyes, but then boarded and spent the night on board with his men.

Cleo gave Antony an experience he would never forget. He would be served by Egyptian servants who would serve him some of the most delicious foods he had ever seen. Of course, Antony's officers also could partake in this lavish banquet. Cleo was seated at one end of the huge dining table in a rather enigmatic, gold engraved chair. There was a broad variety of food. The options were endless. Bread, butter, and all kinds of vegetables. Beef, fish, and cheese. All the men who sat at the table were astounded by the queen's god-like appearance.

She came sailing on her large ship and had everything she needed. It was as if her whole palace was with her on the ship itself. Antony commended and thanked Cleo for her hospitality. Then the next day, he joined Cleo in a more private room so they could discuss other diplomatic matters. Cleo told Antony that she had really tried to give respite and help to an ally in Syria. Antony believed every word she spoke. Cleo even persuaded Antony to get Arsinoe IV executed at Esphesus for the part she had working together with Ptolemy XIII. Cleo couldn't risk and didn't want to risk running into Arsinoe ever again. Nor could she risk that she somehow escape her banishment. Cleo didn't hate her only living sister, but she also didn't want any other failed attempts from Arsinoe every time she tried to betray her. Cleo at first didn't know how much influence she had over Antony, but that was only because he was infatuated with her.

Of the three days Cleo spent in Tarsos, she found out on the last day that Antony was in fact in love with her. Cleo asked herself, what was love? The love she had for her son. That kind of love she had for no one else, not even Charmion and Eiras. According to Antony, he had fallen in love with her when he had seen her for the first time during the time when Cleo was fourteen years of age when she accompanied her father back to Egypt. Allegedly at the time, he was a young cavalry officer who was under the command of Gabinius. Antony kissed Cleo's hand. But Cleo didn't want any romantic relationships. Ever since she had to be with Caesar and since all the men in her family were liars, she somewhat despised men. The only boy she loved was her son. Cleo withdrew her hand and said her goodbyes. Antony wanted to follow Cleo, but he was blocked by two Egyptian guards. The next day Cleo told Antony that if he ever wanted to visit Egypt, he would be welcome to do so. Mark thanked Cleo and then disembarked the ship with his men. Cleo then left and went back to Egypt.

41 BC, Alexandria, Egypt: Another year passed, another year that Cleo ruled Egypt with her six-year-old co-ruler son Caesarion. Cleo was rather annoyed at the moment. But that was only because the man she had seen a year or so ago was now headed towards Egypt. Cleo offered to invite him to Egypt but only because she would be rude if she didn't offer anything in return for his assistance in helping her. Charmion and Eiras in this one year were now upper-class citizens. Cleo wanted

her friends to have a good life. They had both been her servants for a long time and so for their loyalty, she offered them a life where they could still be friends, but they could have their own homes and families if they so wished. Her friends at first didn't want to leave Cleo's side. But after some time, they noticed that their new lives and social status gave them more opportunities. Being a friend of the queen would have its own benefits. Cleo was now in her own room, reading through some old dusty scrolls she had found in the library, when she came across one that she had never seen before. This scroll was more like a collection of scrolls bound together by some thick string. Cleo opened the knot and unwound one of the obscure scrolls.

In this scroll, Cleo found a compendium or collection of drawings of creatures she had never seen before. They were definitely not of Egyptian origin. There were creatures with pointy ears, creatures that resembled wolves, and creatures that had the tails of the fishes that swim in bodies of water. The descriptions for the creatures were written in many different languages of which Cleo could recognise some but she could not recognise or decipher all of the languages she came across. Cleo was too curious to stop searching through all the scrolls she had found. Who would forget about these most valuable and interesting scrolls in the library? Cleo thought.
Cleo was obsessed with these scrolls. The scrolls were titled 'ta mystíria ton mythikòn ònton' which meant 'the mysteries of mythical beings'. Cleo was glad to be able to read Greek. Cleo started delving into the mythical world, she saw creatures with wings, creatures with fangs, and one that resembled a horse-like figure. But none of the creatures spoke of the cat people. Bastet definitely was right in that Cleo was again the first of her kind and now, with her two friends and her son Caesarion, she would spread her knowledge of the cat people to whomever she trusted. Whoever compiled these scrolls was a scholar of sorts, a know it all, someone who knew a lot of the world, someone fluent in many different languages and knew of many cultures. This person would have probably travelled through different countries to collect these vast important pieces of information. Cleo decided to hide these scrolls somewhere close so that no one had a chance to take them from her. Someone entered the room. It was an envoy who spoke for Mark Antony.
'Antony has arrived in Egypt, he thanks you for the warm, spectacular welcome he received when he wasn't even in close vicinity of the Egyptian city. He requests an audience with you, Your Highness.' The envoy bowed once and stood there like an intrepid twig as if he was waiting for a reply.
'I will meet him at the Library of Alexandria,' Cleo replied hesitantly.
The envoy bowed once more and left the room. Cleo knew that one

day she would see this Antony again. This man had been haunting her dreams ever since she had met him the first time. Cleo would not admit this to anyone, but she somehow was intrigued by this man. He always was there for her when she was in trouble. He mostly did whatever she asked without question. To Cleo, it was now obvious that she did like Mark more than she realised, but she could never be with this man. Cleo, if she ever was distressed or disorientated, would reveal her true form that of a cat woman. This was made clear to Cleo when she was spotted by her own sister when she was asleep at night and partially transformed. She couldn't be with someone who would or could jeopardise her own and her family's existence. What was to happen if she accidentally scratched or fatally injured Mark while she was asleep? How would he react? He can never and will never understand! Cleo planned to maintain a diplomatic relationship with Mark Antony but that is all that would ever be. Maybe a true friendship and alliance but otherwise nothing more or nothing less. Cleo now ventured towards the Library, where she from the distance could see that Antony was already waiting for her there.

41 BC, Library of Alexandria: Mark Antony smiled when he saw Cleo approach him. He couldn't believe that he was in the company of the woman he so desired to be with and truly loved. But he could sense that for some reason this same kind of love was also not reciprocated by Cleo. Antony always had problems with women, he already had been married multiple times, but he never felt like he could truly be himself with them. He could only be himself with Cleo. He had just married another woman a year ago. The sister of Octavian. Regrettably, Antony also didn't feel at home with Octavia. She was a woman he had married as a matter of convenience and necessity in order to raise his own social status. If he hadn't married her, Octavian would have declared war on his country. Cleo made Antony feel like he had a purpose to fulfill. Antony had to fill this gaping void he had. But Cleo didn't feel the same way he did. Cleo accompanied by Antony showed him the wide halls and large ceiling of the library she cherished so much. Mark could see the liveliness in her eyes when she talked about the library. But then when there was nothing more to talk about other than diplomatic matters or wars, Cleo started stuttering and muttering words Mark couldn't understand or comprehend. Cleo's mind was at war with itself. She didn't know whether she should tell him what she was. For some reason, she felt like she had some kind of connection with him. A connection she couldn't understand. Cleo decided to show him the scrolls she had found a few hours ago. She had been forced to trust him the last couple of years and he had never betrayed her.
'What is wrong Cleo?' Mark asked in a worried tone.

'There is something I have to show you,' Cleo replied.

Mark didn't try to question Cleo's strange behaviour as he tried to trust that she knew what she was doing. Cleo grabbed his hand and they both went back to the palace. Many servants, guards, diplomats, and Cleo's friends were questioning Cleo's unacceptable behaviour. But she was queen so who were they to question her decisions. Cleo and Antony arrived at Cleo's room. Cleo went towards an old parchment where she had hidden the other scrolls about other mythical beings.

'Please come here, have a look at this and tell me what you see,' Cleo asked nervously.

Mark moved closer to the scrolls and saw all the mythical beings that were depicted in drawings. Each had their own specific description and almost all were written in different languages.

'Do you believe in unusual, otherworldly creatures?' Cleo asked.

'Well, I believe in my own gods of course and I idolise some of your Egyptian gods as well. For instance, the sun god Ra,' Mark said carefully.

'Do you believe such creatures as shown here could have indeed existed?' Cleo continued to question Mark.

'Do you mean exist here on our plain? Flesh and blood? Here physically speaking?' Mark was confused by Cleo's queries.

'There are things here written on these pages that even I can't comprehend. For instance, what is an Alv? I can recognise the letters but not actually what is written here. There are languages here in these scrolls that I can't even understand. What I am trying to say is ... if a creature like me exists, then why can't these also be real?' Cleo said.

'What do you mean by creature?' Antony asked.

Cleo wanted to answer the question when Eiras and Charmion entered the room.

'What are you doing here ...?' Cleo managed to say when she was intercepted by Charmion.

'We are a creature you won't find in those scrolls,' Charmion said. Cleo anticipated that Charmion would now reveal her true form. Charmion and Eiras both transformed into menacing looking felines and they both, with their glaring eyes, stared and hissed at Antony.

'That's enough!' Cleo shouted.

Both Charmion and Eiras reverted back to their human form.

Cleo could notice that Mark had sweaty palms and that he was nearly about to faint. He had been leaning against a table the whole time.

'I ... I do not know what to say. So, you are also this kind of creature?' Mark asked in an embarrassed tone.

'Yes, I am, I have much to explain. But for now, you look like you need to rest,' Cleo said.

'It is just a lot of information to wrap one's head around. It is now obvious to me that creatures do exist,' Mark said.

Cleo was concerned that Antony would now faint, so she helped him towards a comfortable seat and let him stay with her for the night.

The following day Cleo was now sure that Mark was to be trusted
as he could have shouted for the guards who stood guard down the
corridor. Mark was still snoring in the chair Cleo helped him too.
Cleo, as quiet as can be, tapped him on the shoulder.
'Marcus Antonius you may now wake up,' Cleo said sarcastically.
Mark awoke and grinned at Cleo. Cleo was now reassured that
Mark was indeed on her side. Cleo could somehow sense this now.
'Come on the day is young. We have many matters to discuss,'
Cleo said encouragingly.
'Could I have a tour of Egypt?' Mark asked.
'Yes, of course, Alexandria, the Nile, anything you wish to experience or
see,' Cleo replied.
Cleo was about to leave the room when Mark had one last thing
to ask, 'So, what can you do? What powers do you possess?'
'We have a lot of topics to discuss. You just found out that I am
a creature. Come on let's have a great tour of Egypt first though,'
Cleo replied.
In a short duration of time, this friendship turned into something
more and Mark accepted Cleo for who she was.

37 BC, Alexandria, Egypt: For the last thirty-seven years Cleo called
Alexandria home and yet much had happened over the last three years.
Cleo had another two children one named Alexander and the other
named Cleopatra. Cleo loved her sons, but she loved her daughter to bits
since she was the only daughter she had. Caesarion loved having a
brother to play with. So, in his point of view, he won either way. Antony
as always was away fighting wars and gaining back new territories for
Cleo and Egypt. Cleo though was fed up waiting for him to show up. She
hadn't seen him in three years. The last time Cleo had seen Mark was
when he left Egypt in 40 BC. They both had confessed their feelings for
one another, and he went away to get back territories Egypt had lost to
the Roman Empire. Cleo didn't want him to leave straight away since she
had just found out that she was yet again with child, but he didn't want
to listen as he was determined to get back what Egypt had lost.
Caesarion was now ten years old. He seemed more sure of himself than
ever. Caesarion may have looked like Cleo, but he had the same
determination, headstrong and confident temperament like his father.
Cleo was about to go to Alexander and her daughter Cleo's room where
she would tell them the story she was told when she was a little girl.

Cleo could see that they both were tired, and she decided to now
tell the story: 'Once there lived an ambitious man named Alexander
the Great. He was determined to travel the continents to find new

regions, people and map out a dynasty of sorts. We are descended from him, as his only true sister, who was also named Cleopatra secretly married our ancestor Ptolemy I Soter. The first Ptolemy our founder was a general alongside Alexander. When Alexander tragically passed away, our founder Ptolemy took Egypt (Alexandria) for himself. So, as the story tells us, we are all descended from a great Greek hero and explorer.'

Cleo could see that the little ones were now fast asleep. Cleo left them alone and made her way down the corridors towards her own room where she still as always was investigating the secrets of the mythical scrolls. Three years ago, she found an inscription which read Aristotélis in Greek which meant Aristotle; this signature inscription was on This meant that the great Aristotle, a Greek philosopher who was the teacher/tutor of Alexander the Great of Macedonia, was fascinated by the deep mysteries of the world. That was all that she had found out since. Cleo had been mostly preoccupied with raising her twins and making sure that they were well-educated even if they were only three years old. But first things first Cleo wanted to ensure that little Cleo and Alexander would meet their father. This would be the first time they would meet him. Cleo received a scroll the next day. It was Antony. He wanted to see Cleo. Cleo laughed, it was as if he could read her mind. Mark requested her to meet him in Antioch somewhere in Turkey.

It took Cleo a few days to arrive there. When she saw Antony she ran towards him and hugged him. A servant walked slowly towards Mark with the twins one in each hand.
'And who are these little ones?' Mark asked confused.
'These are your children,' Cleo said.
'My ... my children. Well, what are their names?' Mark replied.
The twins blarbed, 'Alexander and Cleopatra. Mummy, can we go home?'
Mark smirked as he couldn't believe his eyes. Antony was happy to see his family once more. The family he just now found out he had. Cleo could notice that something was troubling him. Cleo followed Antony to a tent where they had a one-to-one. Antony would confide to Cleo that he would need further support in the Parthian war with King Herod. Cleo granted him further resources, Egyptian soldiers, ships, and whatever else he would further require. On that day, Antony gave Alexander and little Cleo their second names. From then on, they would be known as Alexander Helios and Cleopatra Selene. Helios in Greek means Sun and Selene means Moon. Mark could notice that the twins were tired, so he told Cleo to put them to bed. He also bid Cleo good night, but Cleo decided to spend the night with him.
Cleo was also more content because her two children had finally seen their father. Cleo didn't stay around for long though. She discussed

future matters with Mark the next day. Matters which involved their children. Alexander could possibly marry into the Armenian Royal family so that he would be king of Armenia, and they had other plans for little Cleo. Cleo left Antioch so that Antony could continue his campaign. He told Cleo he would think of her and the twins the whole time. It would be as if they were there with him wherever he was. Cleo, on the way back to Egypt, shed a tear as she wouldn't be returning to Egypt with Antony.

36 BC, Alexandria, Egypt: Caesarion was waiting for his mother to return from Antioch. She had again been summoned although she was with child and heavily pregnant. Cleo returned back to Egypt within a week this time though she was accompanied by Antony. Caesarion was happy to see his mother and also Antony even though he wasn't his real father. Two weeks later Cleo gave birth to another baby boy whom they named Ptolemy Philadelphus. Antony was proud to be father to another boy. Cleo only was happy to see Antony smile. Little Cleopatra Selene though wasn't particularly interested in the whole commotion. Cleo was glad that her whole family was now together again. Cleo told Antony about the things she had found out from the scrolls over the last few months he had been away. She had found out that the fanged being was called a Vampir which came from somewhere in Eastern Europe, what it was she didn't know. She also discovered another being called a capall uisce with a picture of a horse in a body of water, but she couldn't decipher what the word meant. For some reason, Aristotle must have known someone would find these scrolls so he translated them into languages not everyone could understand so that only specific countries could find out the meaning behind the words. Cleo told Antony that she might not be the one to piece this scroll together but someday somebody would. Antony told Cleo to rest because she had just had a really long and difficult day. Cleo did rest and dreamt that she herself one day could unravel the secrets of those scrolls.

34 BC, Egypt, Alexandria: With age, Cleo became an older and wiser woman. She taught her children whatever she could and tried to be a good role model for them. Caesarion was now twelve years of age, the twins were both six years, and a little mischievous toddler Ptolemy was almost two years old. Cleo tried to teach her children how to control their mythical form. You would just have to focus on one specific thing, a memory, a feeling, and then use one of your powers. Alas, little Cleo was the best at using all of her powers, but her brothers weren't that far behind. Little Cleo whom Cleo also called Selene was the only child who behaved mostly like Cleo and this year Cleo gave Selene the one item she cherished the most, the

small carved wood figure Bastet which she had gotten from her own mother. Cleo's sons Caesarion and Alexander took after their fathers. A year ago, Antony left again for Armenia and was again engaged in a war of sorts. Cleo though knew in her gut that he would return soon enough.

A few weeks later, Mark returned to Alexandria. He had a defeated look on his face. Cleo tried to cheer him up, which seemed to work for a while until he was reminded how much Octavian hated him. Antony told Cleo how much propaganda was being circulated in Rome, about how he had already married Cleo illegally even though he was still married to Octavian's sister.
'They are saying that you are brainwashing me, which is most certainly not the case. I am in love with you!' Mark shouted.
'That is all that matters,' Cleo said.

33 BC, Egypt, Alexandria: In the last year or so Cleo only then noticed how she had been neglecting the closest friendships, Eiras and Charmion. Cleo awoke from a deep sleep. She had dreamed a dreadful thing had happened which was luckily not the case. The dream that Cleo had involved her dear friends Eiras and Charmion who were drifting away into an endless night. It was like this was a sign telling Cleo to reconnect with her friends. For seven whole years, somehow Cleo had forgotten all about them. Probably because she had been focused so much on her own family and her problems that she forgot about them. Ever since they had transformed into their mythical form in front of Mark Antony to show him that mythical beings truly existed so that Cleo herself wouldn't have to jeopardise herself in case Mark had reacted differently. Cleo felt guilty now, guilty about herself and guilty because of the fact that she had let down her friends. They must have been content with their new lives and status that they themselves had their own important things to think about. Cleo left her room leaving Mark alone. She touched the clay walls of the corridors and looked at the hieroglyphs that were carved into almost every wall. Cleo called on her servants to assist in dressing her and afterward, she asked one of her envoys to send an invitation to Eiras and Charmion to come to the palace. The envoy left the room and Cleo would now wait for this highly anticipated meeting with Eiras and Charmion.

A week passed and Cleo was still waiting, waiting and waiting.
Cleo decided she would go to them if they wouldn't come to her. Cleo dressed in a veil of sorts so that she wouldn't be harmed so much by the sun's rays. She would take her daughter and younger son Ptolemy with her. Two guards keeping watch on either side. Cleo ventured into

Alexandria's upper-class village where she was told by a few common folk people where Eiras and Charmion were supposed to live. Funnily enough, Eiras and Charmion lived side by side in clay, mud-brick houses which had a flat roof surface. Little Cleo was muttering about with herself the whole time. She had the tendency to talk to herself and her imaginary friends whom she gave made-up names. Ptolemy, on the other hand, who was now three years of age, was being cradled in Cleo's arms. For the last few days, he had been screaming about something he would only see at night. He complained that he saw some sort of figure which resembled a cat that would sneak around his room while he slept. Cleo never caught a glimpse of such a creature. She only thought that it could have been Caesarion who as of recent had liked playing pranks on his younger siblings. Cleo knocked on the door and was now awaiting Charmion or Eiras to answer the door. But to Cleo's dismay, a little girl about the same age as little Cleo appeared before her.

'Who are you?' the girl asked in a curious tone.

'Skaara, Skaara where are you, I told you not to open the door to strangers!' Eiras shouted.

Eiras couldn't believe that Cleo stood before her. Cleo could see that Eiras was angry with her daughter.

'Shar'e please help me, your daughter has again disobeyed me!' Eiras said.

A strong built man with dark hair came and grabbed Skaara's hand. All Cleo could hear as they walked off was, 'Can't you for once listen to your mother?' Shar'e said to Skaara.

Eiras turned around to face Cleo.

'What begs your appearance at my front door?' Eiras asked casually.

'I am so sorry. I know so much has happened. I am trying to make up for it now. Please ... forgive me,' Cleo said remorsefully.

'I do not know what to say. I would have come to the palace but ever since I married, I have had other things to protect and think about. I myself am sorry. I hope that we do not drift apart again,' Eiras replied.

Cleo was relieved to hear these words from Eiras.

'Now who are these little people?' Eiras asked curiously.

'This is little Cleo, and this is Ptolemy,' Cleo said.

'Ah, now how many children do you have?' Eiras mocked Cleo.

'Too many to count. I am just teasing you. I have as you know Caesarion, little Cleo, Alexander, and Ptolemy. I have four children now and now I have had enough of them,' Cleo said sarcastically.

'I know what you mean, and my hands are full with one of them. As you yourself can see,' Eiras said.

Cleo knew indeed what Eiras meant especially since her dark black hair looked all puffed up and electrified.

'Do you know if Charmion is home or not?' Cleo asked.

'She isn't home currently, she is at the markets with her two children,

a girl and a boy. Her husband is a delegate for Egypt at the palace. You should know him, his name is Teal'c,' Eiras said.
'I didn't even suspect that he was married to Charmion. Thank you for your time and honesty. I shall now return to the palace and come back another time to visit Charmion,' Cleo said.
'You don't have to leave. You can stay with us while you wait for Charmion,' Eiras replied.
'I do not want to intrude, but if you don't mind, I would love to catch up with you about what has happened these last few years,' Cleo said.

33 BC, Alexandria, Egypt, Eiras's house: Cleo reminisced with Eiras about past times. While little Cleo and Skaara played with one another. Ptolemy had fallen asleep in Cleo's arms.
'How old is your daughter?' Cleo asked.
'She is six years old. Full of imagination and stupidity,' Eiras said.
Cleo laughed.

'I am sorry it is just she sounds a little like my daughter Cleo. She as of recent has been talking to herself for some reason. She keeps speaking to a little boy named Darius and a girl named Roma,' Cleo said.
Eiras sat there like a frozen statue. Eiras didn't have a pale complexion, but she did now.
'What is wrong?' Cleo asked.
'How ... how is that possible? Has your daughter ever met these children?' Eiras tried to say at the same time she was gasping for air.
'What do you mean? Are you saying you know these children?' Cleo said in a frustrated voice.
'Well, those are the names of Charmion's children,' Eiras replied.
Cleo tried to make sense of a situation that made no sense at all.
'Cleo has never met these kids. What is going on?' Cleo said.
Both Eiras and Cleo looked at their daughters in utter disbelief.
Cleo knew that this had to be more than utter coincidence. She knelt down next to the children and started asking her daughter a few questions.
'Little Cleo, is there anything you would like to tell me about your friends?' Cleo asked.
'My friends are my friends. Why are you so interested in what I do all of a sudden,' Little Cleo said.
'Well, your friends are in fact real people. Are you aware of this?' Cleo again asked.
'Of course, I know they are real. We talk about everything. We are real close. Roma, Darius, and I. Can you please stop calling me little Cleo, can't you call me Selene instead?' Little Cleo said.
'Okay, Selene. I apologise for calling you little Cleo,' Cleo said.
Cleo wanted to get up when Skaara tugged her veil. Cleo knelt back down.

Skaara whispered something into Cleo's ear.

'I also hear voices. Darius and Roma. I also speak to other people with weird names, Caesarion who keeps telling me to leave him alone, Alexander who talks to me about his stupid war games and little Ptolemy who keeps screaming all the time. I also speak to Selene who in my opinion is the only sensible person I talk to. Do not tell my mother I ever told you this because she will think I am insane,' Skaara giggled and continued playing some game with Selene.

What Cleo just heard meant that Selene wasn't the only one in the family who heard voices. For some reason, Caesarion and Alexander never told her about these psychic conversations they had, and Ptolemy was too young to understand or comprehend who he was hearing anyway. Maybe they thought she wouldn't understand. Cleo told Eiras the complicated situation they found themselves in. Eiras couldn't at first believe what she heard, but then she remembered that Skaara once talked in her sleep about a person named Selene. Something strange was happening and it was up to Cleo and Eiras to find out what was going on.

33 BC, Alexandria, Egypt: Eiras could hear that Charmion had finally arrived home. Cleo left the house with Eiras and left the children under the care of the guards and Shar'e, Eiras's husband. Eiras knocked on the door. They could both hear heavy footsteps. The door opened and an older, bald, serious looking man stood in front of them.

'Ah, Eiras thank you again for that lovely fish dish you prepared yesterday. Who is this?' Teal'c asked.

'This is our queen; don't you recognise her from the Egyptian court?' Eiras said.

'Oh, I didn't realise I am so sorry. Come in, who am I to refuse you some of our humble hospitality,' Teal'c said in an embarrassed tone. Cleo didn't care if he recognised her or not.

She needed to see Charmion sooner rather than later. Cleo entered a house that was larger than it looked from the outside. She could hear Charmion's voice in the distance.

'You have to learn this so you can one day follow in your father's footsteps,' Charmion shouted.

Charmion left her son's room and then came across Eiras and Cleo. Charmion started to laugh uncontrollably. Cleo didn't understand her old friend's insanity. Charmion thought she was looking at a ghost. She hadn't seen Cleo for a rather long time, so Charmion thought she had been hallucinating. Cleo tried to persuade Charmion that she was in fact standing there physically. After Charmion knew Cleo was in fact real and not a figment of her imagination Charmion calmed down, but now there was an awkward silence. Luckily this quietness didn't last long. Eiras told Charmion that Cleo had regretted not seeing or visiting them for the past seven to eight years and that is why she was here now. Charmion tried to believe Eiras but she was more sceptical about Cleo's appearance here in her own home.

'I do not want to intrude or disturb you. But there is another matter that I also must discuss with you concerning our children,' Cleo said in a nervous voice.

'What does anything have to do with my children? Why the sudden interest in my life or that of my children?' Charmion said in a demanding tone.

'I am sorry ... so sorry but I have come to believe that our children are somehow able to communicate with one another telepathically,' Cleo said.

'How is that ... how preposterous!' Charmion shouted.

'It is true, if you do not believe Cleo, please believe me. My daughter Skaara has also been acting strange lately,' Eiras said.

Charmion gave in, it seemed that whatever was troubling Cleo was also wreaking havoc in Eiras' life. Cleo followed Charmion to Darius and Roma's rooms. Darius was reading some kind of scroll whilst Roma was scribbling on a small papyrus piece. The boy was a really confident but stubborn-natured child. The girl Roma though had a playful and imaginative temperament. Cleo tried to ask the girl some questions and soon found out that she had been communicating with Skaara. Charmion couldn't believe her ears. Roma knew things about Skaara she shouldn't have been able to know of. Darius and Roma had played with and met Skaara. These meetings however didn't happen very often. Eiras shouted for Cleo to come to Darius's room. Cleo and Charmion went towards the boy.

'Your son, Charmion, has been talking to me about a girl named Selene. This also happens to be Cleo's daughter. Do you need any more proof Charmion?' Eiras asked.

'That shouldn't be possible. How did you get such powers? When do you remember first talking to these other kids telepathically?' Charmion asked her own son.

Darius spoke, 'The first time well ... was about ... I don't know exactly when. But she came to me in a dream and in this dream ...' Darius was about to say when he was interrupted by Cleo.

'Who came to you?' Cleo asked.

'You know who, Bastet the goddess of health and fertility. Like it says in the hieroglyphs. In this dream, she told me that I was the next step in evolution and that I ... I would be bestowed the gift of telekinesis. Afterward she showed me that I wasn't the only one she granted these powers, in my dream I met Skaara, Selene, Caesarion, Alexander, little Ptolemy, and of course my sister Roma. All of us thought it was a dream until we could also communicate with one another during the day. Of course, we thought you adults wouldn't believe us, so we hid these newfound abilities. I am sorry to keep this secret from you, Mother, but Bastet told us to tell no one of our power,' Darius said in a worried tone.

Charmion told Darius that she wasn't mad with him or Roma. She was glad though that Bastet had not done anything to harm them. Cleo though asked herself why her children were sworn to secrecy by Bastet. Cleo spent the night at Charmion's residence where she decided to reconnect with her friends.

The next day she went back to the palace with her children. Tonight, she would plan to summon Bastet. Cleo tried so hard to summon the goddess she used to idolise so much. But it was no use. Bastet still didn't show. Now Cleo was unsure though whether she could trust Bastet anymore. Cleo bid her daughter Selene and son Alexander good night. She went to Ptolemy's room where she would keep an eye on him for the night. Cleo sensed or had a hunch that for some reason Bastet was keeping Ptolemy awake at night and she had to find out why. Many, many hours passed and the candle that had illuminated the room now had dimmed down. Cleo was about to fall asleep, but she was determined to find out what happened in Ptolemy's room during the earliest hours of nightfall.

33 BC, Alexandria, Egypt, Ptolemy's room: The room was now dark, with the only source of light being the full moon outside. Cleo could hear a scratching sound it was coming from outside Ptolemy's room. The creature came into the room but from what Cleo could make out she could see it was only a typical house cat. For some reason, Cleo thought that the cat was Mau. But how could that be? The cat would have to be more than twenty years old! The cat tried to grab Cleo's attention by jumping on her lap. Cleo pushed the cat away from her and before her eyes, the cat transformed into Bastet. Cleo couldn't believe her eyes. The cat she knew as Mau had been Bastet all along. 'I wish you no harm. Nor do I want to cause harm to your children. I just want to ensure that my legacy. Our legacy will last forever. It shall be a dynasty spanning thousands of generations. I have lost this chance before, but I will not lose it again. This is our dynasty of cat people and that is why I have bestowed these powers on our next generation,' Bastet said.

'What do you mean by powers? I am only aware of one power,' Cleo replied.
'Your children and their friends have the ability of telepathy and the power of astral projection,' Bastet said proudly.
'What is astral projection?' Cleo asked.
'Astral projection allows the person who is asleep to separate

themselves from their physical body. Meaning that when your son Ptolemy is dreaming, he can go wherever whenever he wants without being seen. This gives your children the power to be anywhere at any time,' Bastet tried to explain to Cleo.

'Why do they have these powers and I do not?' Cleo asked.

'I apologise for my indiscretions with your children. I didn't mean to keep it a secret. But I knew you would find out about their powers eventually. I am also sorry for not telling you this before ... You don't have these powers because these abilities progress, evolve, and grow stronger with time and since you were the first of this dynasty you, unfortunately, do not possess these powers. I have bestowed these extra powers also because I believe someday that your children will be in danger. So, I helped them grow stronger so they wouldn't be so vulnerable to any threat that could come their way,' Bastet said very fervently.

'I am grateful for your honesty. But I sometimes do have my doubts about your motives. I do not care about any powers. I just wanted to know why you did what you did,' Cleo said.

Bastet looked at Cleo when her eyes suddenly glowed. Cleo awoke the next morning, she could remember the events of last night, but if felt more like a dream than anything. Ptolemy for some reason was already awake.

'Mummy why do you talk to cat lady?' Ptolemy asked.

It was now evident to Cleo that what she had experienced last night was far from a dream.

32 BC, Athens, Greece: After a lengthy discussion Cleo had finally persuaded Antony to send his wife Octavia an official declaration of divorce so that she could finally be married to the man she wanted to be with for the rest of her life. Cleo and Antony left Athens for Alexandria. Once they were back, both were exhausted from their journey and so they went to sleep early. The next day Antony left Egypt for another war that had been started by Octavian. As of recent Octavian had found and revealed/made public the contents of Antony's will which stated the following:

-Caesarion is to be the next Caesar of Rome.

-I am to be buried next to Cleopatra in Egypt and not in Rome.

-Alexandria will be made the new capital of the Roman republic.

By making the content of Mark Antony's will public, Octavian declared and waged war on Cleopatra. The reason for waging war was more or less because of Cleo's territorial acquisitions which were to someday be her children's lands. Another reason being because of the military support Cleo gave to Antony. Octavian now had the support of Rome, and he was coming for Cleopatra and her children. Cleo felt like she was standing on the edge of a cliff and was about to fall off. Cleo had an uncanny feeling she couldn't shake off. In the last few days, Cleo thought about that night one year ago with Bastet where Bastet told her that she had bestowed these powers to her children because she thought her children would be in trouble someday. Cleo didn't want Antony to leave because she had a bad feeling about his leaving. She couldn't change his mind though, because for Antony, waging war against Cleo meant waging war against himself as well. Antony was determined to keep his family safe at all odds even if it meant risking his own life. Once he was gone. Cleo was planning her next move. Cleo summoned Charmion and Eiras to the palace as there was a lot to be discussed.

31 BC, Alexandria, Egypt: Octavian was creeping up closer and closer to Egypt. Cleo had seen this with her own eyes since she had accompanied Antony on one of her ships in one of the battles, they both faced against Octavian. Cleo lost many fleets and ships since many of Cleo's people weren't suited to combat in this sort of this situation while Octavian's men were trained for this specific kind of warfare. Cleo could see that she was slowly losing the battle against Octavian so she readied herself, her friends, children, and followers for the worst. Cleo didn't want her children to end up as pawns in Octavian's game or her friend's children, so she was going to enact her plan as soon as Octavian was in close proximity to Egypt.

31 BC, in what is known as winter in the Northern hemisphere; Alexandria Egypt, Royal Egyptian Palace: Cleo was preparing to be invaded by Octavian. She was preparing herself and her children for the inevitable. As part of the plan, Cleo would be looking for identical-looking children to that of her own so they could take the places of her children. It was all part of the show. Because once Octavian would arrive in Egypt, he would try to take her children as well as herself with him to Rome. What Octavian didn't know is that he would in fact not be taking the right children with him. He would fall into her trap as he would take these fake decoy children in place of her right children who would hopefully have made their way far away from Egypt.
Cleo's children would ask her what was wrong and why she was trying to replace them to which Cleo would reply, 'I am not trying to replace you. One day you will come to understand the choices I have had to make to keep you safe. You won't be alone, you will have some friends to keep you company.'
Caesarion was the only one not willing to listen to his mother.
He was now seventeen years of age, and he was determined not to leave Egypt in Rome's hands. He firmly believed Egypt was his legal birthright. What he didn't think about was the fact that if he stayed, he would probably only risk his life instead. Cleo couldn't get Caesarion

to agree with her instructions so instead Cleo sent him to enter the ranks of the ephebi. It was a tradition for past pharaohs to enter the ranks of the ephebi. The ephebi was a sort of school/college for young men aged seventeen – twenty-five years of age where they would learn the art of survival, learn more about politics, and immerse themselves more in the lives of commoners/public. Caesarion wouldn't be going alone. Mark agreed to his son Marcus Antonius also joining Cleo's son in the ephebi. Cleo would be worried about her son but she had other children to think about as well. She also didn't want to prohibit Caesarion from making his own decisions since he now was almost an adult and would want to have and learn from his own life experiences. Cleo now in a list ditch effort decided she would send Octavian a message which she would give one of her envoys.

This letter would state the following:
*I know I am speaking to the one who is now in power and to
the man who has the upper hand in the dilemma I now find
I now in a show of solidarity offer you immense
of amounts of money in the future. I am also sending you a
gold necklace, which has the Egyptian sun god Ra engraved
on it. In return, I request that my children's lands be returned
to them, and that Mark Antony should be allowed to live in
exile in Egypt. If my demands aren't met, I will burn myself
with all my treasures in my tomb before you can even get here.
Queen Cleopatra
of Alexandria, Egypt*

Cleo knew that her chances were slim that Octavian would even consider any of her demands. Especially since she wrote such a naive letter. Cleo though knew that Octavian would react to this letter and that it would tug at his heart strings because she had threatened to burn all her treasures and that is not what he wanted. Antony also sent Octavian a message, but he received no reply. A few weeks passed by, and Cleo received reply back from Octavian in the form of a papyrus letter with the Roman seal. Cleo was trembling all over as she carefully tried to keep the letter from falling out of her hands.

She started reading the letter she had received from Octavian, but this letter consisted of only one sentence:
*I, Octavian, ruler of Rome, shall invade Egypt and nothing,
nothing will change my mind.*

Cleo was pacing back and forth in her room. She was enraged and concerned at the same time. All she could do now was hope that the plan she had started would work and, as she stated in the letter, she had sent Octavian, she would now gather all her possessions, jewels, and works of art in her tomb so that she would be ready for whenever Octavian was to appear. Cleo had to make sure she would be ready in the event he were to appear almost immediately so she would send spies to Antony's camp so she would be the first to know when Octavian would make the first blow.

30 BC, July 24th, Alexandria, Egypt: For the last few months Cleo tried to enjoy the company of her friends who were in fact looking after her real children. She would never though trust herself enough to visit her children since she didn't want to reveal their true location in case Octavian had spies of his own and so most of the time she would be alone in the palace where she only had the company of Teal'c, the husband of Charmion. Cleo trusted Teal'c with her children, her plan, and her own life. Cleo could sense that he was a man true to his word and so he was a great ally to have. An envoy appeared accompanied by one of Cleo's spies. Cleo asked the envoy to leave as she wanted to speak with the spy in public. It seemed that according to this source of information that Octavian was about to battle against Mark's inexperienced cavalry and naval fleet. Cleo knew what this meant. She gave her informant a few gold pieces and asked him to continue his job. The informant for some reason didn't want to leave though.
Cleo asked him, 'I have asked you to leave. Please heed this instruction.'
The person wore some sort of thin cloth around the head, they didn't reply but started to remove the head covering instead. Now a woman stood before Cleo. A woman Cleo had never seen before.

There was something peculiar about her. Something different like she had an essence surrounding her. In a matter of seconds, the woman transformed into a leopard with the greenest eyes Cleo had ever seen and then back again into her human form.
'Wow, what kind of being are you?' Cleo asked curiously.
The woman replied, 'I am a sorceress of sorts who dapples in all sorts of wonderous magic.'
Cleo was impressed by the magician and asked her the next question,
'I do not mean to be rude but what is your name and what is your reason for being here?'
'Well, I need something ... I mean something which only you possess. One is a key ingredient for a spell, and one is something you hold dear. A document that contains information about many mythical creatures. Not to forget, my name is Inari.'
Cleo had so many questions which circled her mind but one she thought would be the most important. 'What do I get in return for the things that you want?'

'I offer you and your family protection and also this handy device. It is called the seeing eye, it has two specific functions, it can show other mere mortals who is a mythical being and reveal their other form. The other is that if the phrase, 'All is as can ever be' is said then this device glows and destroys the user's enemies. Be careful not to forget the phrase though, otherwise it is useless,' Inari explained.

Cleo tried not to touch the seeing eye glass pyramid with her bare hands so that her mythical form would not be revealed. She placed it down on her table and retrieved the bunch of scrolls she had found a few years ago. She handed them to Inari. Cleo could see that Inari was pleased with the scrolls she had received. But there was one other thing Inari also wanted. She wanted a drop of blood from Cleo.
'A drop of blood from a feline predator,' Inari said in a mischievous tone.
Cleo tried to trust Inari and so she cut her hand and Inari held a vial to get the blood. Inari put the vial away and then asked what Cleo wished for her to do next. Cleo herself didn't know how to proceed further. She was certain that Mark was going to fail against Octavian's now immensely larger forces and so she proceeded to write a letter.

If you read this letter now, then I am probably dead already.
Do not fret about me as I have done all I can do. Save yourself
while you still can.
Yours forever, Cleo

Inari asked Cleo why she would send Antony a suicide letter to which Cleo already had an answer, 'Because he would otherwise give up on his children. Without me, he knows he needs to be there for his children.'

Inari didn't know what to say. She only thought that Cleo was a complicated, maybe at times smart woman. Cleo ordered Inari to give Mark the letter the next day. Inari left the room and was given a place to stay in the palace.

30 BC, August 1st, somewhere outside Egypt: Octavian had just defeated Antony's naval fleet and cavalry. Antony tried to hide himself on his ship. He hoped that he would be able to get away even if his chances were low. While he was sitting somewhere on board the ship in a cramped space, a woman appeared out of nowhere. She told him that she was ordered to give him a letter. Once he had read the letter though, Antony did exactly the opposite of what Cleo thought he would do. He stabbed himself in the stomach. 'What a complicated relationship,' Inari said to herself. Antony was distraught. He had just lost the one true love of his life and so he wished to no longer live. Inari decided to take

55

Antony with her as Cleo would be rather angry if she left him here. Inari teleported with Antony to the Egyptian palace. A dying Antony was now lying in Cleo's room. Cleo had just returned to her room from a meeting she had with her other diplomats. When she saw Mark, she knelt on the ground and asked Antony what had happened. Mark looked at Cleo with a sad and confused expression.

'I thought that you killed yourself. Why ... why did you?' Antony said.

'Stay quiet Mark. Is there anything you can do Inari?' Cleo asked.

'I am sorry but there is only so much my magic can do,' Inari replied.

Mark grasped Cleo's hand and told her, 'Octavian will be here soon, save yourself and the children. While you still can.'

'I will, I will,' Cleo replied.

In this one hour, Cleo didn't let Mark go and tried to keep him comfortable for as long as she could until he took his last breath. Cleo cried as she had never done before.

'Why did I write that stupid letter!' the queen shouted.

Cleo had to come to understand that there was nothing she could do for her dead husband. She pulled herself together as her plan would need to be enacted now.

Cleo ventured towards her tomb with the seeing eye. Then she sent two of her envoys to get Charmion and Eiras. Cleo was ready to burn everything to the ground. She was relying on Shar'e and Teal'c to get the boats ready. Cleo ordered her servants to pile wood in front of the palace and then burn it so that Octavian could see the smoke cloud from far away. Antony's body was embalmed, organs removed, and then placed in Cleo's tomb. The smoke cloud outside would act as a distraction so that Octavian wouldn't notice anything suspicious going on. Cleo would have used the seeing eye, but it was useless to her because she had forgotten the phrase Inari had told her about. Cleo put the seeing eye somewhere in the tomb. She didn't care if it was destroyed. Charmion and Eiras rushed to Cleo's aid. They both knew what would happen if they stayed in Egypt, but they were always loyal to Cleo and would never let her down. Both Eiras and Charmion had already said their farewells to their children since that would be the last time they would see them alive. Cleo was standing in her tomb and now at least she wasn't alone as Eiras and Charmion were by her side. They waited until Octavian had arrived in Alexandria.

He proudly announced to all Alexandria's people that Egypt was now under Roman rule. Octavian could see Alexandria's people despised him, but he knew that if they dared harm him that they would only pay the price instead. Octavian went for the bait that Cleo had put in front of him. He could see smoke clouds emanating from the palace and he thought that Cleo had indeed burnt everything he so very much wanted. While Octavian wasn't aware, Teal'c and Sha're were gliding past him on two of Cleo's trade ships. Cleo and her friend's children were hidden under the fishing nets and under piles of food. They were accompanied by many common people and servants who acted as if they were fishermen. Cleo's plan for now at least had somewhat succeeded as Cleo's children had escaped unscathed. Of course, Cleo didn't know this for sure as she was still waiting for Octavian to show. Cleo at least knew that Inari had somehow spellbound the ship so that no one would be able to see it. Another few minutes passed and now finally Octavian found Cleo. Cleo, Eiras, and Charmion were seized and trapped in a room whilst Octavian thought that he had also captured Cleo's three youngest children. Cleo was in a state of shock. She tried to think of past times, just a few days ago Caesarion had returned from the ephebi. Cleo had sent him to upper Egypt so that he would be at least for now out of Octavian's reach. Cleo didn't know what would happen next and so she remained trapped in the room with her friends until the next day. The next morning Cleo was greeted by Octavian's ugly face. He seemed content having captured the queen and her children.

'You didn't think you could win against me!' Octavian proclaimed.

Cleo stood there in silence, all she gave Octavian was an empty glare so that he didn't think he had conquered her.

'Now I will let you also parade through the streets like your sister Arsinoe and your children will grow up to be upstanding Roman citizens.'

'I will not be led in triumph!' Cleo said and spat at Octavian.

Octavian grinned and left them alone. The Roman guards escorted Cleo and her friends outside where they could overhear Octavian talking with his diplomats.

'Caesarion has gotten away!'

'We will deal with him at another point in time.'

Cleo could also overhear them talking about a trade ship that had just left two hours ago. They had some nice fish and beer on board. Octavian ordered a few of his men to intercept the ship so they could get some more food here. Octavian asked where that ship was headed. Another voice replied towards Greece, another towards South Africa. Either way, Octavian didn't want that ship to leave anytime soon. Cleo couldn't listen to this ranting any longer.

She turned away as she whispered into her friends' ears, 'I no longer care what happens to me. Will you help me destroy Octavian?'

Eiras and Charmion agreed to help Cleo which would be the last thing they would ever do.

Cleo and her friends turned into three dark black feline monsters. With their teeth, they would try to bite anyone they could hurt easily. With their claws, they would kill anyone who got in their way. They pounced on every guard and diplomat until only Cleo and Octavian were facing each other. Eiras and Charmion had passed on as they had been struck by spears during the whole massacre. Cleo sensed Octavian's heartbeat going faster and faster. She was ready to pounce on him when, unfortunately, a spear got Cleo from behind. Piercing her heart. In a matter of seconds, she was deceased. Octavian was as pale as the moon. He couldn't believe his eyes. Cleo's body turned back into the human form. Now the last long ruler, Queen, Pharoah of Egypt was dead. Octavian now journeyed back to Rome. Taking Cleo's fake children with him.

A few weeks later a young Caesarion
was deceived by Octavian. Octavian told him that he would be able to rule Egypt. Caesarion, now Ptolemy XV, would reign for a mere eighteen days until executed on Octavian's orders on the 29 August 30 BC. Octavian would, later on, be known as Caesar Augustus. Selene, Alexander, and little Ptolemy had successfully escaped from Egypt. Where they would now go was another matter entirely. Inari the sorceress left as soon as she had upheld her end of the bargain and now the children were under the care of Shar'e and Teal'c. Cleo, Eiras, and Charmion would always remain by their children's side, in spirit of course. Selene would never forget what her mother had sacrificed to get her and her siblings on the ships, she held her most prized possession so tightly, the carved figure of Bastet she had received from her mother. For a few months, they travelled south then east towards the unknown. At one time though the two ships that travelled together were split up. One ship ended up in what is now known as the Amazon forest in South America and the other somewhere in a then-unknown continent Australia.

This was indeed the start of a dynasty of cat people.

Cleo's body was also mummified and put next to Antony in the tomb. Her organs were put in jars in a large stone box with the seeing eye. At one instance in time, Cleopatra's tomb was infiltrated and a rainstorm that also damaged the tomb washed many artefacts including the stone box into the Nile.

Thus, this ends the story of a woman who truly was the last ruler, pharaoh, and queen of Egypt who has left an enduring impact on

Egypt and that is her legacy.

Word Glossary

The Seeing Eye:

A rather peculiar device that the OGR has in their possession. It is a triangle like, opaque and slightly see through structure with a stone set in it which is called the 'Seeing Eye' and if a mythical creature touches it, it reveals their true identity/form. The Seeing Eye also has the Egyptian Seeing Eye in gold colours on top of its glass surface.

Would our other books be of interest?

Find out more on our website:
www.seeingbeingsisbelieving.com

Or find us on Facebook.

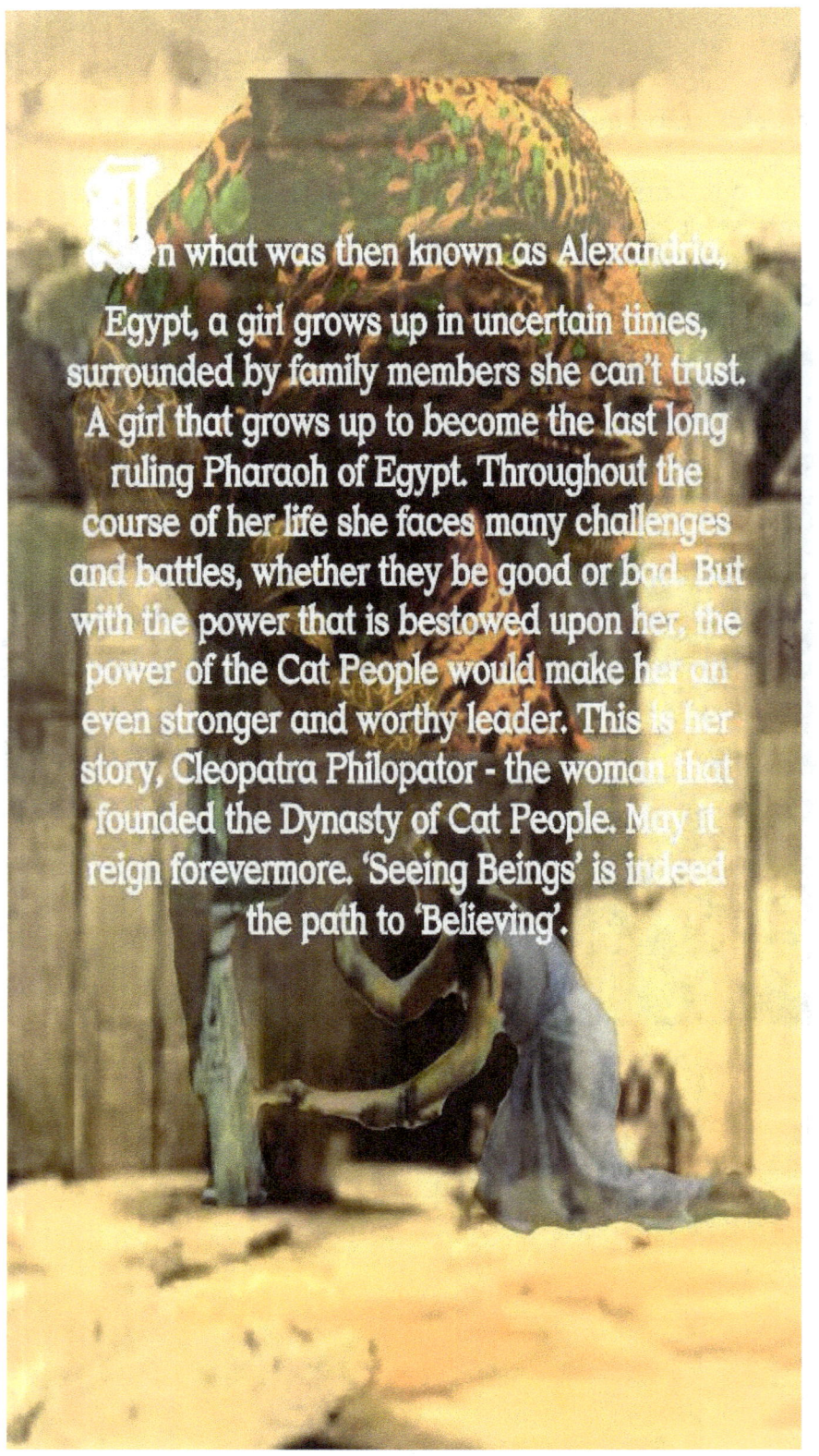

In what was then known as Alexandria, Egypt, a girl grows up in uncertain times, surrounded by family members she can't trust. A girl that grows up to become the last long ruling Pharaoh of Egypt. Throughout the course of her life she faces many challenges and battles, whether they be good or bad. But with the power that is bestowed upon her, the power of the Cat People would make her an even stronger and worthy leader. This is her story, Cleopatra Philopator - the woman that founded the Dynasty of Cat People. May it reign forevermore. 'Seeing Beings' is indeed the path to 'Believing'.

www.ingramcontent.com/pod-product-compliance
Lightning Source LLC
Chambersburg PA
CBHW061138200626
46817CB00016B/2059